Follow Your Heart
Wait upon the Lord

By

Grace True

Grosvenor House
Publishing Limited

The right of Grace True to be identified as the author of this
work has been asserted in accordance with Section 78
of the Copyright, Designs and Patents Act 1988

This book is published by
Grosvenor House Publishing Ltd
Link House
140 The Broadway, Tolworth, Surrey, KT6 7HT.
www.grosvenorhousepublishing.co.uk

This book is a work of fiction. Any resemblance to
people or events, past or present, is purely coincidental.

A CIP record for this book
is available from the British Library

ISBN 978-1-80381-804-7
eBook ISBN 978-1-80381-805-4

Dedication

I give thanks to the Lord
for my angels: Lawrence and Ophelia
and for a special friend.

But those who hope
In the Lord
Will renew their strength.
They will soar on wings like eagles;
They will run and not grow weary,
They will walk and not be faint.
Isaiah 40:31

Praise the Lord
for He is Good!

Contents

Chapter 1   Start walking again   1

Chapter 2   The memory   16

Chapter 3   At the hospital   32

Chapter 4   Further away   51

Chapter 5   What shall I do?   64

Chapter 6   Wrestling with God   73

Chapter 7   My Mum went to heaven   82

Chapter 8   Shall I be with you?   91

Bible References   107

Chapter 1
Start walking again

It was a beautiful day of autumn and today was my day. It ended up to be a day that I would never forget. It was better than my usual nights. I found the nights harder and harder to go to bed and sleep. It was harder and harder to deal with each night as the nightmares were slowly putting me down. Two days up and three days down was not much I was doing. The doctors, well, how can they really help? They did try all sorts of things. My friend Dennis told me I should try something new. Well, I was not taking medication anymore but doing some sort of therapy and was not helping me. Seemed to me I was just talking about my dreams. It felt stuck and not having a fulfilled life. Why? Sometimes some questions did not have answers and sometimes it seemed impossible, however I was moving forward and kept going. Not sure how but I was not the type to give up easily or to feel defeated by life and its ups or downs.

I was a solicitor after all, and had done pretty good in my life. At least at the career level.

And when you think where I started, I really came a long way. You could say I dedicated my life to who I became today and it was a slow long process and following from studies to training, all kinds of policies and procedures and a job which I enjoyed and kept going up and up on the career level.

Took me years of dedication and patience with perseverance to be where I was and was offering me in a way financial security and a job that I really enjoyed.

"Are you coming?" I heard a voice behind me. It was my mother. She was living with me as I was looking after her. Maybe she was looking after me in a way. My brother Paul did not want to look after her and had a good excuse as he was living 3 hours away so I ended up looking after my mum. Her name was Ana. But I would not have wanted any other way as she was so dear to me and I loved my mum so much. Guess both of us had to deal with the same issue and that was loneliness. We both felt lonely but living in the same house, it started not to feel so lonely anymore. Anyway my mum could not afford living on her own anymore and was too much for her in some days and found it difficult as she was not so young anymore. But to me she always looked young and lovely.

"I am coming mum!" Just give me a minute.

She was at the main door waiting for me and I was not ready. That was happening every time and she kind of knew it by now. Looking three times in the mirror, I looked good. My dark hair was looking

2

good and my blue eyes sparkled. I had a nice shirt and looked smart. I always looked smart dressed.

"You are not going to the court, it's just Church!" she smiled looking at me with love.

"I am coming, mum, I am coming." was rushing out the door.

Then as I helped her entering into the car I added:

"How did I convince myself of this going to church idea, I am not sure, but there you go. At least you will leave me alone, hopefully for a year!" I laughed.

She looked at me and pretended to be upset, touched my cheek with love.

"You need healing, Jason! Your dad did a lot of damage to this family before he died and only Jesus brought me peace. You need to find Jesus. I keep telling you."

"I think God needs to find me, I am too much in my own busy world, not sure I have time for him, mum!" entered the car and was ready to drive.

"That is the problem, He always has time for you, and he loves you. You need to make time for the Lord."

"One good thing, I started to love going with you to church and meeting lovely people. Seems like a very kind, peaceful environment. Totally different from fighting in court!"

We always had these conversations and I knew the Jesus path or the way and I was very excited about it, however that was when I was a child. As I grew older I felt Jesus was not there for me and was not answering my prayers and was so angry with the Lord.

But the Lord was always there and trying to reach me.

Never understood much of the paths of the Lord.

But yes, my mum kept telling me He was there, but that's not how I felt. I wanted it my way and everything that I was praying about to happen right at that moment.

My mum was right, I was angry with my father as he hurt our family so much. Well, my father died many years ago drinking too much. And then I was just 10 at a time. That seemed a long time ago. But wounds heal hard and scars can still hurt.

As I drove after 20 minutes I was in front of a beautiful church building and had a large entrance. It was a big charismatic church and was here where my mum started going for so many years, all since my father died.

As I entered the building a few familiar faces said hello to me and of course they recognized me. My mum was always helping with all kinds of church groups and she had her little group of friends, all lovely ladies that were very chatty and they met weekly for a coffee and a cake.

A lady approached my mum immediately as we entered:

"Ana, glad you brought your handsome son, otherwise he would have never come. He is so handsome, and tall!"

They all looked at me with admiration.

Was true, I was actually a tall guy, 6'1 and yes, that was me. Very confident and very bold, but polite, kind. I worked hard to get where I was and was a pretty good solicitor working in a prestigious firm: Sunrise Family Law Firm. Now I was a senior partner and was working there since I was 22, and then was more than 15 years.

Yes, I was 37 years old. That was me, Jason Wright.

We all sat down and soon enough the service started.

The preacher was saying something but I did not listen much or if I did, I felt tired. All the same things to him that Jesus saves, forgives, loves, heals, restores. Mostly than anything when I went to church I felt emotional. Why would I go with my mum? But I promised her that each month I would go twice. It was quite a lot for me. But she was my mum and wanted her to smile and stop nagging me in a way. I was in my own world and was afraid to let anyone into my heart. Probably was too complicated or I was making my life too complicated in a way.

Today I was a bit tired as I had another nightmare last night and I wished my mum would have let me stay at home and rest as I could not sleep much. The service finished quicker than I thought. As I was walking toward the main door to leave, lots of people were going and coming and talking. I turned around quickly to see where my mum was and just bumped into a young lady that dropped a lot of papers on the floor.

"I am so sorry, please forgive me!" I spoke and leaned to help her pick them up.

As I was helping the lady to pick up the paperwork, I could see her beautiful face and I was very close to her. She smelled of roses:

"I am Jason!" I smiled and she raised her eyes and I could see her beautiful green eyes looking at me and a lovely blondish hair:

"I am Audrey!" and she stood up to leave.

"Ah, I am sorry!" I was a bit lost and did not find the words, but really wanted to talk to her.

"Is ok, Jason. Nice meeting you. I have to go to the kids groups! See you later." and she left smiling shy at me.

As she was leaving I felt admiration in my heart for her. She had something special and could not tell what. In a way it was early days to say like this, as we just met.

On the way home, I ended up very chatty and my mum was so happy as she always was the one talking, especially when she went to church. Her heart was there, her friends.

My friends asked me to go to the pub with them tonight: The Red Bull, our favourite place but I was too tired and probably I would not go. Lately I was mostly at home and could not go out anywhere. My mind was still at Audrey and wanted to explore more about her and know more about her.

"Who is that lovely lady that works with kids: Audrey!?"

"Yes, she is a nice young lady, she is very good with children."

And my mum wanted to change the subject and talk about her own thing and I was a bit impatient:

"... and Audrey, what else about her?"

"She is a lovely lady, she is always in church. She is a nurse."

My mum was back talking about one of her own ideas.

I knew there was no point mentioning to her about Audrey as I would not get more information from her at that moment in time till she would finish her stories. So I dropped it for the time beign.

It was quiet in our home and my mum went to rest in the afternoon and I crashed on a couch. As soon as I reached the couch, I fell asleep.

I had a dream that I was on a road and that it was dark. And next to me was someone walking and I saw this girl Audrey and she did not say anything. As we were walking it seemed that the night was becoming morning and the sun was rising and we kept walking and on a hill we saw someone there waving at us and we started walking there.

A loud noise woke me up and it was my phone, probably ringing for some time. As I picked it up I heard my close friend saying:

"Hey, sleepy head, hope I did not wake you up, again? The boys are going to the pub as you know but I am staying home with my love, so if you want to come for dinner, let us know. We do not want you to always be alone!"

I stretched and looked at the clock, it was 3 pm and yes, I must have slept for 2 hours.

"Yes, that would be good, I think I am passing the boys this evening, will drop them a message."

"We kept chatting: Lucy and myself that we do need to find a girlfriend for you, as otherwise we will hire you as a babysitter when we have kids." and he laughed.

Dennis Taylor was my best friend and he was working at a big Company - a firm that was doing software. He has been my best friend since high school and amazingly we managed to keep going in spite of the years passing. We were a small group of friends, mixed jobs and we met over the years and became friends. We used to meet for barbecues and we kept in contact with each other.

As I was ready to leave for Dennis' house, a few hours later, I felt in my heart, I would better not go and just take a walk.

Was not sure why but followed my heart. The park was not far away from us, like a 15 minute walk. I picked up my phone and texted Dennis that my plans changed and I would not come for dinner. Dennis was always so good and understanding, did not say a word and was probably used to me always changing the plans.

I told my mum I will take a walk and she approached me and looked at me concerned:

"Are you alright Jason? You rarely take walks like this, unplanned. Usually you are running in the morning!"

"Yes, you might be right, but that is what is on my heart today!"

As I started walking, I felt fresh air and for the first time in a long long time I looked at the birds and the air and felt the nice breeze. It was 5 already but I did not feel hungry!

As I was walking a few people said hello and I even stopped to speak with the neighbour. Well, I loved chatting with people, but some days I was a grump and forgot how to interact as much in my own world.

Suddenly I saw a car parked in a nice area, and it was a nice little red BMW. As I was thinking to pass it by, I noticed the same smell of roses and turned my head. That moment I saw the lady from the church: Audrey.

She turned her head the same time as I turned mine and our eyes met. She smiled and put her head down shy.

I stopped and turned around and started walking toward her:

"Hello Audrey! How are you?"

"I am fine, thank you. I just visited my grandmother."

She was dressed in a lovely pair of jeans and a nice red t-shirt. As I looked at her, she seemed a bit shy, but a kind, nice lady. She was not very tall, slim and had a beautiful smile and lovely green eyes. She was glowing for some reason and I could not say anything.

For a moment I just looked at her and the solicitor, knowing all of me, felt lost, without words and did not know what to say to her or how to speak with her.

"Are you going for a walk?" she asked.

"Yes, I was thinking of going for a walk, would you like to join me?"

She looked at me surprised and she did not know what to say.

"I… Jason, it is late!"

Looking at her, I smiled but realised she was getting shy and confused with me. Well, I had an impact on many people, not only in court but in real life. Probably too direct and charming at the same time.

"What do you say, if I will take you for a walk and dinner."

"But, I, … you must…!"

I was not planning to give up and was waiting for an answer getting my confidence and being who I was:

"Come on Audrey, you know my mum and you know a few things I am sure about me. I will not run away with you!" I laughed.

She started to relax a bit and looking at me curious added:

"All right Jason, let's go for a little walk and a little dinner. I did not have any plans tonight, so, why not!"

As we started walking she looked at me and started the conversation:

"You are working as a solicitor, aren't you?!"

I looked at her and for a moment she stopped and I spoke so serious:

"Yes I am a family solicitor, working for the "Sunrise Family Law Firm", Jason Wright!"

Then I started laughing:

"Jason for you!" and our eyes met again and this time, I felt shy, which I never do.

"You are really funny, you know!" She smiled at me.

"Well I do not want to scare you, but yes, in my past years of work, like 15 I saw quite a lot of broken hearts, families, pain and hurt. In my own way, I try to make a little difference in this world the best I can! Trying to make a positive impact in people's lives is not easy when they just want to fight and are all broken and they need a way out."

"That is kind of you!"

We walked a bit in the park and then as we were getting to the other side of the park we noticed a small restaurant.

"Shall we eat there, we both spoke at the same time!" and we laughed.

"So, where do you work Audrey?"

"I work at the hospital, as a nurse.!" Then she looked down and said with a soft voice:

"Probably not as exciting as yours!"

"I am sure it is a great job, if you like it and you help people, it is good. I could not do it, for sure!"

We sat down to a little table and we ordered:

"I keep seeing you at church, Jason. Do you know Jesus?"

Made a face and looked at her:

"Yes and no, not sure, yet. I know about the Lord and believe in the Lord, but too stubborn and in my own world. My mum keeps encouraging me to come and she has good intentions. But not sure if my heart is fully into all those beliefs. I feel I can't do it as people expect so much from me."

Audrey listened and spoke with passion:

"The Lord is good and kind. He loves you and accepts you as you are!"

She made me feel curious and asked her:

"You think so?" I was doubting.

"The Lord is a good loving Father and accepts and loves you unconditionally, does not love like us, people. Yes, He changed my life and I am not turning back. That was the best decision of my life to follow him with all my heart."

At that point I was not really agreeing with her:

"Not sure if I am ready to follow him. I have so much to deal with in my heart and am not ready to be face to face with a Holy God... you know."

Without any hesitation with a firm but kind voice she spoke:

"Jason, stop running and finding excuses, only the Lord can heal you and help you in whatever you are going through."

The rest of the evening went quiet in a way, as some things she said went straight into my heart. She was not only beautiful but killed me softly with her wisdom, kindness and beautiful eyes.

I had a lovely evening with her and walking back, it started to get dark and I wished the evening would never finish.

The Lord wanted me to take a walk. Look what a lovely time we both had, something I never planned.

Just followed the first desire and prompted my heart to go for a walk. And I had been in the company of a lovely lady and enjoyed speaking with her. The things we spoke challenged me and I would have to store them and think of them.

"Thank you for a lovely evening, which I enjoyed Jason!"

"I had an amazing time, Audrey! Would you mind if I ask for your number? I would like to meet you again.!"

Unsure, she looked at me, and a strong wave of wind passed and she started to shiver:

"It is getting cold!"

In an instinct, but passion and desire to protect, I went near her and put my arms around her. I just wanted to be there for her. Was something that I did following my heart. She was just lovely.

"I am sorry, I do not have a coat, just me and my heart!"

She wanted to get out gently from my arms, but for a moment she did not move.

Looking at her serious I said:

"Will you take my heart? It will warm you up?!" and smiled at her.

We stopped for a moment and she turned around and was in a way in my arms, we were so close to each other and she looked in my eyes:

"You are serious, Jason?"

"Yes, I am! Would you take my heart and look after me! And will you let me look after you!?"

Realising the emotional tension between us she gently got out of my arms and kept walking slowly. Was something that was birthing and a fire that started in our hearts and at that point we felt the emotion of it.

We were walking quietly next to each other and soon we were near her car at exactly the same point we started our adventure today.

"Can I please drive you home!"

"If you insist, Audrey."

She drove quietly and in 10 minutes we were in front of my house. Before I got out I turned around and my voice was a bit defeated:

"Thank you for a lovely evening and walk! I wish I could meet you again, Audrey! You are a beautiful lady and have a beautiful heart!"

As I got out of the car, she said nothing. She got out of the car and she came near me. I thought she would say something like: goodnight and thank you, but she already did that. Instead she did something very unexpected.

She put her head on my chest and her arms around me and held me tight. I could feel her heart beats and smell her hair and she held me tight and just said:

"You are a lovely man, you are loved by the Lord, Jason!"

Then she turned around and got out of my arms that were holding her tight like she was mine.

Without saying anything she looked one more time at me and just drove off.

I did not know what to think or to feel but everything was so different. It was an amazing day for me and since then everything has changed. Probably at that point I was not sure what I was doing and thinking much, but the Lord knew. Later on things would get together as a puzzle missing pieces that were found and making an entire beautiful picture of our lives connected on one road.

Chapter 2
The memory

It was a dark morning of autumn. It was raining and cold and not a pretty day. I was at work and it was so busy! I was going and coming and had to deal with my usual work, in the Fracture Unit! It was something for me that I had been doing for quite some time. I was working on a pattern shift and when I had time I was helping at church.

My life was in a way into a good routine and also had a lot of free time to help at church. As for me and my other side of life, I was sharing a little house with my adopted aunties, both very nice ladies, older than me, in their 50s: Lucy and Clara. They were both sisters going to a very nice traditional Baptist Church.

Or better put it: they adopted me and looked after me.

They had been really nice to me, many years ago, when all it happened. They were an open door from the Lord that changed my life and moved me into the next step and my purpose, the path laid from the Lord.

For some reason as I opened the curtains, it was only 8 am and opened the windows a bit, there was fresh air as it was raining all night and was still raining, small drops falling down consistent and continuous.

The nice voices of the patients told me a nice good morning and I was smiling, being myself.

My big green eyes maybe were the most unusual thing about me. My blondish hair cut on the shoulder level was put up in a bun and had my blue uniform. In a way I was a shy person and reserved but with a kind heart.

Today was another day and I felt sad deep down in my heart, memories from the past were coming back in my mind. That was all long ago, many years ago, but it all happened so quick! It was very painful and sad, like a bad nightmare!

***

Yes, I was a lonely child, lost in a system and not having a place of my own. I was living with my father and my father was … was… I could not even think anymore. He used to come back home drunk, angry and shout at me. No, he did not hit me, so when he was not drunk, he was kind and brought me gifts, but would work so much all the time.

My mum? Can't remember her, I found out she died, and then my father started drinking and working too much. And probably it went like this for a couple of years, I can't remember, till one day he did not come home.

I will never forget the day when a lady from the police came and then another one. Then someone helped me pack and they had a nice chat with me. I was a child of 8 years old or so.

A chat about what?

About life?

But back to reality as heard a voice near me:

"Are you all right Audrey?!" asked Mark, smiling.

He was always there helping me and smiling and he took care of me, helping me even when I needed help.

"I am fine, Mark. I can handle it here. I need help in salon 3."

"All right sweety, salon 3". And he winked at me as he left. Mark and Maria were mostly the nurses I was teamed up with, among other 10, but they became very much a support for me. We were a team. They were both in their late 40s and working in the job for a while. So, I've learned quite a lot from them. And I was the type of person to work hard and not moan, so we all three were making a pretty good team.

***

A voice in the dark was heard and I was alone, and that was my new room. I was not sure where I was, it seemed like a boarding school. I was very shy and quiet as a child, that was me.

And for the first few weeks since I joined, I would be taken after class to meet a lady that seemed very nice but always asking me how I feel and lots of questions. That is how I found out that my father died in a car crash. And me, little Audrey I was alone in this big world and it did seem big to me.

These years passed so lonely and I was a quiet child. Then college and I started training as a nurse. I loved working with people and helping. But my life was so lonely and in a way just found comfort moving with my two friends that they took me under their wing and looked after me in a way like aunties. I was calling them aunties. They were sharing that big three room house and put an ad to take someone else on board to live with them. Their prayers got answered. At that time I was a new nurse, just started working and decided to call them. Immediately they took me in and they offered me love as no-one did before. Probably I never knew what love was till I really really met them.

They were so nice and looked after me. They were working at a Garden centre and their house was full of flowers as well as their garden.

And that was my simple life. My life, with no excitement in a way, or maybe I did not have anyone to share with my day by day goings and coming and working, except my two aunties.

After my years of childhood, the loneliness and all I went through, they were a blessing and a fresh air, peace and a lot of joy, stability and love. They became part of my life and felt really blessed, part of the family. For the first time, I felt I had a family in a way.

They were lovely, however something was missing and I did feel lonely in my heart, missing a heart to beat next to mine, a man!

I was not a child anymore, I was 33 by now and the years had passed so quickly.

For a moment I remembered Jason and for the first time in a long time I enjoyed someone's company in a different way. I have not been on dates in years and can't even remember. I was always shy and reserved and quiet.

Yes, I really liked Jason, and it was nice to be in his company. But he was a bit of a solicitor in a big world. I was a nurse in my own small world. No, probably he just got bored and asked me out, to fill in his time. It would be better to forget him. But I wondered if he was thinking of me and for sure I had a deep desire to meet him again.

As the day passed he still was popping in and out of my heart and mind.

Maybe he was a bit in my heart and I was trying to fight it.

Home, Lucy and Clara spotted me right away that I was a bit too much on the thinking side and being quiet.

They approached me the moment I entered the door.

"Come, on girl, what is going on? Did you have a hard day?" asked Lucy.

Clara had red hair and a very tall figure when on the other side, Lucy was short, funny and giggled a lot. They were the Martin sisters. They never married, and were just enjoying a quiet life of working and helping at their little church. They were lovely and were my aunties, my family. My adoptive aunties. I was repeating those things to myself a lot and they were bringing me comfort.

"Well, I met a nice guy yesterday and we went for a meal and a walk. I know him from church, he comes sometimes with his mum."

Lucy giggled and looked at her sister:

"Aww, there might be hope for our little girl to get married, that is great!" clapped her hands.

I looked down and spoke:

"No, no marriage, not for me. I was just thinking that he asked me for my phone number and did not give it to him.! I wished I would have given him my phone number."

Interrupting with her funny voice:

"Why not?" spoke Lucy.

"Come on girl, for sure you won't get married like this. You need to be nice and you should have given him your number." Clara looked at me seriously and I got back into my shell.

As I went to bed that day, I felt sad. Both my aunties were nice with me and actually cooked dinner, but in my heart, I was wondering if I would ever meet Jason again.

Maybe I will never see him again, except at church, with his mum.

Maybe they were right, I should have given him my number and did not. And those beautiful words he said to me:

"His heart!" Yes, he wanted to give me his heart and how he held me tight. Yes… yes.. I had a sparkle in my heart and smiled sadly. He was a very nice man with a lovely character and handsome, intelligent and with a lovely heart.

But then the same thoughts of No came back to me: "It is not for you, not for you, Audrey!"

***

The week passed quicker than I imagined and here I am Sunday at church, again. For some reason I felt anxious and at the same time excited. Maybe I was going for the wrong reasons at church, to sit down and chill out and also to see Audrey. I did know a bit about Jesus and loved going to church, but now I had another reason, to see that beautiful simple, shy girl that fascinated me with her eyes. And yes, I will never forget the day we spent together and how lovely she was. Her kindness and beauty enchanted me.

I listened to the service and managed to actually be more interested and my mum took care of me. Actually, by now, all the church knew I was a good solicitor, her amazing son and she kept bragging about me in a way. She would make me feel embarrassed sometimes, but she was an amazing mum raising me and my brother alone. I guess in a way she was proud of me.

As I was ready to leave and was chatting with some guys I just met, I turned around and bumped into a lady and she dropped all her papers down.

I leaned down to help her and I apologise:

"I am so sorry!" and stopped. My eyes got big and looked at her.

It was Audrey and she was probably as surprised as me.

"Hi, Audrey!" I smiled, getting back to my normal self.

"Hi, Jason!" She got shy as our eyes met.

"We keep meeting like this, don't we?"

"Yes, we do!" and she was ready to leave when I took her by hand gently.

"Might be a sign from the Lord! Please let me take you to dinner!"

"I, I … Jason, don't know!" and she put her eyes down, shy.

"Please, Audrey, I will pick you up from your grandma's house, 4 pm. Please say yes?" waited to see if she would actually agree.

She lifted her head and looked straight into my eyes:

"I would love to go out with you, but just as friends."

"Of course, Audrey! That's a good start. See you at 4 pm."

My heart got filled with such joy, it was not the joy of the Lord, it was joy to meet Audrey and that she accepted to meet me, again. It seemed to me much easier to win a case in the court than to get out for a meal with her. It made me laugh having that thought.

For years I forgot the smell of a woman and forgot what it is to be around a woman. But Audrey was so special. Something about her, a sparkle started to get formed into my heart. And I was willing to follow my heart and I felt quite excited even if it was not yet a date. I was still meeting her and we were going out for dinner. At this point in time I was not ready for a date anyway.

As I drove back from the church I spoke with my mum:

"What do you think of Audrey, mum?!"

This time my mum looked at me a bit curious. She was always a gentle lady but pretty firm in her own way. Well she raised two stubborn boys: me and my brother Paul, so she had to be firm with us sometimes. We were always wrestling and laughing, a mixture of brotherly love.

"Come on, Jason, tell me, what are you planning? You already asked about Audrey and you don't ask a lot about ladies."

She was still looking at me and I turned my head for a moment as I was driving and smiled:

"I actually asked her for dinner, just as a friend, but she accepted. I will pick her up at 4 pm from her grandmother's house."

"Yes, she does not live far from us!" continued mum.

My mum looked at me wondering:

"You really like her, Jason?"

"You know mum, in so many years, just focusing on work and career, for the first time her kindness and being so sweet just got my attention. She is in a world totally different from mine, but seems more happy than me. She is like a flower that has not bloomed yet."

"And what about Victoria Adams?"

The question really surprised me.

"Oh, Victoria, is Victoria. Just another solicitor in the branch. I am not interested in her, you know that." It quite annoyed me in a way my mother's comment.

"But she seems to be interested in you."

"She is always interested in someone that can make money or help her career, sadly."

I dismissed it and just thought, how lovely it would be to meet Audrey again.

Later on the same day, my friend Dennis called and asked how am I and same question which was asked weekly:

"Are you coming for dinner or any plans?"

"No, I am not, Dennis. I'll catch up with you later in the week. I've asked this lovely girl I told you, this amazing lady that I met, for dinner."

Denis laughed:

"A date for Jason!"

"No, it is not, we just met as friends." but deep down in my heart maybe I wished it would be a date. Yes, in my heart a hidden desire was to go out for a date with Audrey.

Dennis seemed a bit sad, but said:

"A relique like you, will take time to be discovered,... but you are a treasure. Glad you are meeting someone nice. Let me know if you fall in love," he laughed.

"You know Dennis, if she treats me the way she is, probably I will, she is just lovely."

"So, what's her name, this lady you meet?"

"Audrey!"

***

The afternoon came and I was ready. It was so dark outside, but at least it was not raining. I drove to Audrey's grandmother's house and knocked on the door.

A lady with white hair opened the door and smiled and invited me in, but I did not want to disturb. But in the end I decided to step in and the lady, who was Audrey's grandmother, started talking with me.

"Hello Jason, I've heard a lot about you, Audrey is my lovely lovely granddaughter. We found each other after a long time. She is so sweet, always looks after me. I am Martha Jones. Come in young man, come in."

Audrey heard the door and spoke from upstairs:

"Nana, is everything all right?"

"You have a charming young man here waiting for you. So, don't make him wait too long, sweety."

"Ohh, of course, I'll be down right now."

As she came down the stairs she was shining. She was wearing a lovely blue dress and smiled at me. She was beautiful and time stopped for me or I wished it would stop.

"I… you… You… are so beautiful Audrey!"

I felt a bit embarrassed as I had no flowers or anything like chocolates, and just said politely goodbye and under the protective eyes of Martha, her grandmother we entered the car then left.

"I am so sorry, I forgot to buy something for you, I am sorry!"

I looked at her, feeling quite embarassed. How was that possible for such an organised guy like me. Well, it happened.

She smiled and spoke with her kind voice:

"Is all right Jason, your company will be more than anything else I want."

Was not sure what to understand and looked a bit confused.

It was a precious night and we talked about all kinds of things and she laughed a lot. Actually I laughed too and enjoyed myself. I forgot the time and everything around me.

"I am so happy you came today to meet me, you are so special and lovely. Tell me more about you, let's talk about your childhood."

Audrey smiled and a sadness came on her face.

"Raised without a mother as she passed when little, my dad… my dad.."

She stopped and for a moment I did not know what to do. I stretched my hand and got her into mine and held it tight and she carried on:

"My dad was suffering, lonely, working too much,... too much drinking. One day, he was gone. A car crash and I ended up in a boarding school, in the system."

Was quiet and was not sure what to say:

"I am so sorry, it must have been so hard for you."

She looked at me trying to smile:

"Then about 10 years ago, two lovely ladies, in their 50s now, Clara and Lucy took me under their care, in a way. I was searching for a room to live somewhere as I was a new nurse and they took me in to live with them. Not only me, but they also loved me and are my adoptive aunties. They helped me find my nana Martha."

It was quiet for a moment and then after few more words I asked her:

"Have you dated before, Audrey?"

"Long ago, Jason, long ago. And there was only one guy."

Unexpectedly she asked me:

"You must have dated a lot!"

"Had a girlfriend when I was young, but no, did not afterwards as my life became career oriented. And gave up on women and dating in a way."

We both seemed not to push the subject deeper and wanted to change it as you could sense the emotions overwhelming both of us. I felt quite embarrassed sometimes and not sure how to treat her and behave around her.

It was late and we were both tired. We had been over 3 hours in the restaurant and we were talking more than eating.

On the way back, it was windy and cold. I offered to take her home.

Clara's and Lucy's house was in another part of the town in a way, but that did not bother me. Was not too far away. I assumed she walked to her nana.

"This is where I live. Thank you for a lovely evening. Was nice to know more about you."

I got out of the car and walked her to the door.

"Thank you Audrey for a lovely evening.

Looking at her the time stopped for a moment:

"You are so beautiful!"

I turned around and wanted to leave, but could not.

"Would like to meet you again, please. I love being with you and …" I took out of my pocket a visit card.

"If you want, I mean… I would love you to text me, call me."

She looked at me and she laughed as at the same time she took a little visit card from her pocket.

"Call me Jason!" and we both laughed.

And before I walked to the car I went near her and looked into her eyes. I could hear her heart beating so quickly. I went near her and touched her hair and kissed her on the cheek and gave her a cuddle.

"Thank you, Audrey. I hope to see you again soon."

She looked at me as I was walking to the car:

"I will wait for your call, Jason."

As I drove off I felt so good and in my heart I heard music. Maybe I was enjoying her company too much.

Well I had to work tomorrow and was busy, but my mind was back going to Audrey and her lovely smile. I could not believe so many years passed and I lost interest in dating, having a family.

Now suddenly out of the blue, when I expected the less, the desire came back deep into my heart, or was rebirthing and really wished I would date Audrey.

Was not sure if she really had the same feelings as me or if she was really interested in dating, but I wished she was.

Slowly I started to fall in love with her, very slowly. I always was very picky, cautious in a way, probably because I had high standards and expectations. But I really loved being with Audrey, in fact I adored her. She was amazing to me. Something buried very deep down in my heart started to re-birth itself and was the desire to be with someone, the desire to date, to fall in love, not to be alone. Well, I never felt very lonely, but since I met Audrey I sensed a bit more stability and in a way, in my life.

I could tell you I even started to sleep better in the night and the nightmares were not so bad. Actually my focus was on something else, was focussed on going to church and Audrey. I have learned to ignore the nightmares and without even knowing it the Lord was healing me slowly. But that was not occuring to me at this point in time, I would realise that at a later stage.

Also deep down in my heart was getting healed in some areas that I would never imagine or think, it was regarding relationships and finding true love.

It was something that the Lord was doing and for sure I had no idea, I just noticed that my life was having a ray of sun and beauty.

I still enjoyed my job but with a different perspective.

A new priority that was forgotten, hidden re-birth itself to a new level of touching my heart to emotion to passion and to open the door in my heart to fall in love.

Chapter 3
At the hospital

It was a lovely morning and a couple of more weeks passed. Jason texted Audrey and she replied. Both of them were looking forward to hearing from each other, it seemed both were at a confident pace.

For some reason his days seem brighter and his colleagues said he looked different. His heart had a different attitude and he felt he would like to meet Audrey and spend more time with her. But no, he did not meet her and she said no past week as she was busy.

The Lord was working at his character and was working new things in his life, He was transforming and renewing his mind.

Hidden steps were revealed as Jason was moving step by step into his destiny with confidence. He never lacked courage for sure, but this was different, a new challenge.

This morning Audrey was working in the morning shift and she was doing her usual things. Suddenly the doors opened and there were a couple of patients being directed to their allocated places.

As she turned around to guide where the beds should be moved and in which saloon which patient, her face got full of surprise:

"Jason! You, here!" and her heart started to beat so fast and got scared that someone would hear it!

He smiled at her and said very charming:

"I missed you so much that I decided to come and see you. Except I injured my leg!" and pointed to his leg making a face.

"How did it happen?" She looked a bit concerned.

"Got hit by a car! Couldn't avoid it in time! The Lord meant it to happen, so I could see you, Audrey!"

She almost whispered:

"That's why you didn't text me.!"

"I was so close to you. I was next door, so, did not have to text you! Couldn't you sense that?!"

As she was leaving she whispered to him:

"I will look after you, Jason!"

He smiled and he ended up in a small saloon with 4 beds. They were empty and he was the only one there!"

Mary called her to help in another saloon and Jason did not see Audrey for some time. He had other nurses "visiting" him as he used to say but he wanted to see Audrey. He wanted Audrey to look after him. Like this, he would have seen more of her.

After three hours she came and did her routines and checks as she was a nurse after all and probably it was her turn.

"Sorry, but I am busy and we work in different sallons !"

Jason looked at her and he smiled:

"I am happy to see you! So you are looking after me now."

She got shy and asked to check his blood pressure and as she was putting the band around his arm she got shy and their eyes met.

"How long do you think I will be here for?"

"Probably after the scan the doctor will decide, depending on the type of the injury, if your bone is affected!"

Jason was so closed to her and took her gently by the wrist:

"As long as I can see you, I do not mind!"

The same time a doctor came in and she left quietly and later on she heard from Mary that he will probably be only a couple of more days.

She left home sad in a way but happy that saw Jason.

Next day she was working an afternoon shift and was anxious all day and her aunts noticed that. They were very sweet and kind and did not embarrass her with questions or annoy her.

Audrey did share with them that Jason was in hospital with an injured leg.

***

All day I had been waiting for her and found out that her shift was only later on. My heart was thinking of her and wished so much to see her.

As she walked the corridor and noticed her beautiful figure my heart started to beep so quickly and was really overwhelmed when she was near me.

The same time another lady was walking behind her: Victoria Adams and when I saw her, I made a face. For sure I woke up to reality from my beautiful dream. Her and Anthony were the last ones I wanted to see. I wished she would somehow disappear from the company as she used to annoy me lately. Well! It worked for a few months, and it seemed she had the mood to annoy lots of people.

As she walked toward me, I smiled but I was not the type of guy to pretend. Anthony was working with me for so long and was my faithful assistant. Probably did not know how to get rid of her. He was a quiet soul, more like living a quiet life. I was the one that had many times to deal with challenges in the company. I started to get used to the fact that my life might never be as quiet as Anthony's.

And I would have not liked it, I was more competitive and loved challenges, I would have got bored for sure.

"Hello Darling!" and she came near me and I kind of turned my head and she realised I did not want a hug, I never did anyway and pulled a chair and decided to sit down. I was not the type to hug women and she tried each time with me and never worked so far.

"Hello Victoria and Anthony!"

Behind her Anthony was making a sign with his hand that he tried his best but could not get rid of her.

"How are you doing? So don't tell me I will take your cases?"

I looked a bit surprised at her and with a very serious voice I said:

"Maybe you forgot that I am a senior partner in the firm and no, "my darling", you won't take over my cases!" I tried to kind of imitate her, kind of being a bit bold and rude at the same time.

Anthony started giggling and she turned her head annoyed.

She was a tall woman and she had long nails and very high heels. She had very high manners and a proud attitude. She got a position in the firm only a few months ago and she was trying to swim her way up, but no one liked her. As many came and went, I was sure she would be the next one that the company would get rid of. Some people want to be paid for not working and being charming.

My phone rang at the same time and I excused myself and she started to talk to poor Anthony who was such a quiet soul and did not know how to handle a very noisy bossy woman like her.

"Hello I answered and I was surprised to hear one of the partners in the firm asking me for a meeting that would be next week to take some decisions."

They wished me all the best as they heard I was in hospital but they said they would send me an email to update me with some points to be discussed and if I had anything to add to send a reply in the next few days. I kind of knew the procedures by now. Not the best to work in a hospital but I always had my laptop with me.

As I hang up the phone, I saw Audrey coming and she excused herself:

"I do need to do my usual checks for you."

Victoria looked at Audrey and made a face:

"Lower class! Go on darling, do your job" and dismissed her with her attitude and voice.

Jason felt his heart melting but did not say anything. For sure he did not like the way Victoria treated Audrey but did not say anything. Over so many years being a solicitor has learned how to be quiet and what to say, what not to say, and when, how to behave in different situations, otherwise you will lose a case. But not only lose a case, words could build up a person or tear them apart.

Many people in pride, anger, pain would say lots of things that were painful and were hurting others without even realising sometimes. The worst cases were when dealing with people that were vengeful and stuck in the past that could or would not move on.

Deep down in her heart Audrey did not feel very well and she noticed she was being analysed and she tried her best to finish her usual checks for blood pressure. She was calm and with precision in less than 10 minutes she finished.

She looked at Jason and said:

"Thank you!" and she excused herself.

After 15 more minutes of torture listening to Victoria and her moans, Jason excused himself and said, that he is tired and wants to take a nap before dinner. He was actually tired and wanted a break and some quiet time.

"Anthony, can you stay 5 more minutes please. We need to catch up."

That tall lady turned around and said:

"Why can I not stay?"

"Well, Anthony is my assistant and works with me, for me, for the firm. I need to talk to him in private, is that all right, darling?" I got a bit sarcastic.

As she wanted to leave, she came near me and before I could react she leaned and gave me a kiss on the cheek. The same moment Audrey was passing by going to the next door saloon to do the check ups for other patients and caught the moment.

I felt so bad, but it was too late. How would I go about explaining that to Audrey?

The time passed really quick and was early bed time for me and she was finishing her shift later, at 9 pm or so.

She came to do last check ups as there were 2 more people in the saloon with me as they came earlier today.

Waiting and waiting she did come to say goodnight to me:

"Goodnight Jason, Mr. Wright!" she smiled.

"Audrey, look… I want…"

She turned around and spoke with sad eyes. I could see that she was a bit bothered by Victoria and her visit earlier.

"Look Audrey, please talk to me!"

"I am working, Jason. Maybe we can talk on the phone later. But I already saw you today, quite a lot."

Looking at her I insisted:

"Can I call you later tonight? What time do you finish, please?"

She looked at her watch:

"Around 10, I should be home and available for you."

"Thank you!"

The rest of the hour I kept looking at the clock and praying, for some reason that I could not explain, praying. When it was 10 pm, I just called her.

Audrey was home with Lucy and Clara around. They were kind of in the background doing things or more like being there as they were a bit concerned for Audrey.

"Hello Audrey!" she did pick up her phone.

"Hello Jason, yes. What is the subject that you want to talk about that could not wait?" she just nailed it.

With a deep breath I got my courage and spoke:

"Today, I had Victoria and Anthony!"

She interrupted me and said quickly:

"Your private life, work, I know, you are a solicitor and I am a nurse."

My heart melted and it was exactly what I did not want to happen and were the words I was afraid she would say to me:

"Audrey, can you please listen!"

Was silence the other side and finally she said:

"All right, Jason, I will listen."

"Victoria came to my firm a few months ago and she is a very bossy proud lady, and sadly she tried to make her own way in a pushy way. She tried that with every guy in the company to get her own way, the way she talks and acts. You saw her giving me a kiss on my cheek. Trust me, I am not interested in her and I tried to avoid it. And Anthony, the guy you saw is my assistant. He works with me, for me, however you want to call it." I was between being calm to agitated and not sure how to express all my heart.

Was quiet and I was a bit concerned that she was not on the line and I asked:

"Audrey, are you still here?"

"Yes, Jason, I am listening, I heard a calm voice."

"Please, please don't think I am interested in her."

It was a long silence and she spoke with a very soft voice, almost fading:

"I am not sure what to think, Jason, about everything."

"Can I please text you, see you?"

"Jason, you are, you are … an amazing man, I… you… Don't know Jason. We can text but give me some time and space. I need time please."

***

Next day when she went to the Hospital he was released unexpectedly and sent home. Audrey got sad. In a way she wished he would not leave yet. But in a way it was better. She was a nurse, working and having a simple life. Jason was such a big solicitor, successful and was not even much interested in God and so many ifs were in her heart, doubts. But at the same time, she was thinking of him, his smile, his eyes, his words and his heart. He was a lovely man, with a kind gentle heart and she enjoyed his company.

Later on when she finished her work she notice couple of messages from Jason:

"Hello Audrey, I have been released and now at home with my loving mum. How are you? Had been thinking of you and believed it or not, even prayed for you. Jason"

She was thinking of answering that evening but decided to leave it till next morning and that is what she did.

She was not sure and felt confused in her heart. Prayers were bringing her peace. She could not move left or right. Clara and Lucy were more like listening and they did encourage her to follow her heart and they even prayed for her.

Another day and she could not answer Jason, than another one passed till soon it was Sunday.

This Sunday I could not go to church and had been thinking maybe to text her again or not. Probably I was each day thinking of that and me, the one that was not much praying I ended up praying for Audrey, probably more than I had been praying for myself.

My heart felt sad and hopeless and gave up thinking or knowing what to do. Was much easier to be in court than anything else. Anyway I had to go back to work on Tuesday and had to do some work from home for the past few days. And Anthony, who was so kind, offered to give me a lift back and forth to the offices for a couple of hours. In a way was a very nice friend, not only an assistant, he was faithful, kind and had a nice wife. And he was not the type of person to complain.

The day passed so hard for me and my mum went to church. She was so kind to me, and felt she was pampering me.

She was spot on to know something was not right.

"Jason, what bothers you, you never seem worried or sad at all. It seems to me that the past few days you have had a sadness in your heart that I can see not only on your face but your behaviour?"

"Yes, mum, maybe. I do not know." tried to avoid her questions and did not want to share my heart. It was enough for me to deal with my own worries and concerns and I liked being in my own castle.

"She came near me and touched my face and gave me a hug."

Few tears started to come down my face but still tried smiling:

"For the first time in a long, long, very long time I like someone and do not know what to do and how to do it, I really feel hopeless."

My mum smiled and whispered:

"Is it Audrey?"

"Yes, it is! How do you know?"

My mum was always a very kind patient mum and loving to me, and always there for me. The past years I just worked and worked and worked. I did not want to stop and did not want to slow down, I just wanted to find my way in life. My heart got lonely and locked in a castle. Now for the first time I wanted to let someone into my castle and know my heart. But at the same time I had fears and did not know what to do or how to do it.

It was an interesting feeling and I never thought of having a relationship. I kind of got used to my lonely life and just work, work work all day long and meeting Dennis or some of my friends sometimes.

Sometimes you can bury your loneliness through work or in other things that surround you. When some people go through loneliness and pain they end up in all kinds of addictions and they do not know how to deal with their challenges. The only one that can heal, redeem, restore and fill your heart with love, joy, peace and can satisfy the desires of your heart is the Lord.

"Yes, Audrey, I would like to meet her. I really like her!"

All the time that my mom was at church, my heart was beating so quickly, I felt so tired, exhausted, even anxious.

I fell asleep on the couch and woke up around 1 pm. My mum told me she had a lift today, one of her friends took her to church and I knew she would be home around that time if she was not talking too much with her friends or was something else going on at church after the service.

And I was right, the main door opened and heard voices:

"Mum, is it you?" and started standing up and had a little stick walking around to guard my leg. It was not broken but was pretty well bandaged.

I started to walk slowly and I was approaching the little hall that was getting to the main entrance and saw my mum coming:

"Did you have a good time mum!?"

As she entered she smiled and looked at me:

"Guess who offered me a lift today?" and she slowly moved out of the way and then to my astonoshment I could see Audrey.

She had a beautiful red dress plain and with small yellow blue flowers and a small blue cardigan and a little bag.

As I saw her was so unexpected that I was speechless and did not know how to react or what to say, just felt so astonished that managed to say:

"Audrey!" and dropped the little stick I had and that moment to get around the house. I literally forgot about my leg and a deep pain hurt me and I fell straight down.

That moment Audrey came near me very quickly and my mum as well.

But she realised that I was in good care and whispered that she will get some rest upstairs and come down later.

"Jason, are you all right?"

I looked at her and she was so close to me and she was smelling like flowers. I wished I could have held her into my arms and told her how much she meant to me.

She offered me her hand to help me stand up and I did not quite want to get her help.

"Audrey, you here?"

Audrey put her eyes down and shy said:

"I wanted to see how you are! I wanted to see you, Jason!"

Looking confused I asked her as I was sitting down the couch:

"But you didn't text me at all, I was waiting for your text!"

I felt so overwhelmed that she was here and was not sure how to behave, what to say, how to speak with her.

"Yes, I know, but that does not mean I did not think of you!"

She asked politely:

"Can I sit down!"

"Of course, please! I can't believe you are here!" and I was still in my world and did not know if I should withhold my feelings or express them.

But what can stop LOVE!?

She smiled and looked at me:

"I am here, or do you want me to leave?"

"No, I don't, please stay! Would you like to have some lunch?"

She refused politely and said will just stay a bit and then visit her nana.

After I recovered from my shock I managed to say few words:

"Thank you, Audrey for coming!"

It was quiet and none of us dared to say much:

"How are you feeling?" She looked at me.

"Much better thank you! I am going to work Tuesday!"

"Is that wise!?"

I looked at her and said it firmly:

"I need to go to work, so much work and I need to catch up. I can not work from home! It is boring as well. The doctor did say I am getting better and it is my choice when I feel ready to start work."

She looked at me and smiled:

"Are you sure he said that? Do you always work so much?"

Out of blue I said something unexpected:

"What else am I supposed to do? I am always alone and do not have anyone to share my life with! And I love my work."

Then I realised that what I said was true. And my heart was so lonely but I was burying myself in the work and kept going, kept going and was missing the joy of life, the joy of sharing and spending time with someone else, a lady like Audrey.

"What about you, Audrey?"

"Since I had been working as a nurse I wished so much to meet someone, but it did not happen. The guys I met, I never felt the Lord saying yes to dating!"

Looking at her I decided to explore the subject and challenge her heart:

"What about me Audrey?"

She got red and her green eyes had sparkles:

"What about you, Jason?" she smiled looking in my eyes.

Took her hand into mine and holding it gentle I asked again:

"What do you think of me, Audrey?"

Turning her head away she did not want to answer:

"Come on, Audrey, we spent a lovely time together, don't you agree?"

With a sad smile spoke up with a soft voice:

"You don't want to know!

"Look at me!"I spoke with a determined voice.

"Yes, I do want to know!" I carried on.

Turning her head she lift her face and our eyes met again:

"You are ... you, Jason, are a solicitor. I am a nurse. I love God and am not sure about your walk with the Lord. You are in a different world than mine and you always work so much. I do not know, honestly. Not sure what to make of you."

My heart got sad as she was speaking more and more and felt hopeless.

"However!"

I withdrew my hand from hers and put my head down. I wished I would not have asked as everything what she said was true and it was painful in a way.

"However Jason, I really enjoy your company and you are an amazing man and wanted to come and see you today."

"That's all!" spoke slowly.

"Yes, why?"

"I thought you liked me, Audreey. I really like you!"

"Jason, I do like you. I came to see you, as I missed you."

Raising my head I spoke upset:

"Then what? You would not go out and date a guy like me? Why?"

Audrey was shocked and for a moment she was quiet. He was still waiting for her reply:

"I want someone that believes in God like me, someone that will be a true husband and we can pray together and our children can come to church. Not someone who goes to church because he dates me or wants to please me! And Jason, your career and work seems really important for you! Could you slow down? Would you slow down? How will you fit a relationship in it?"

Her words went straight into my heart and hit deep:

"You are hurting me, now Audrey!

The truth was hurting me but deep down in my heart I knew she was right. But I did not want to hear it, know it. And for sure not from her.

"Am I Jason? I am sorry, but you asked and tried to avoid talking to you, but this is the truth!"

Was quiet for 5 minutes and I asked her with almost indifference:

"Would you never go out with me?" That was my last hope.

"I did not say that Jason!"

So much confusion and did not understand what she really meant:

"So, what do you want?"

I looked in her eyes and sad did not know what to say:

"I know what I want, Jason. It is you that needs to figure out what you want and then our paths might meet if the Lord says yes for a relationship and we both want the same things."

Few more minutes and she stood up. She looked at me and gently touched my hand.

"I am so sorry if I hurt you!"

"So, you will never go out with me, Audrey?" I still had the same thought.

"You never asked me, Jason and I did not say no!"

I did not move from the couch and could not look at her. She leaned down on her knees and touched my chin. Then I lift up my head and looked at her:

"Sort out your life and heart Jason. Then come and talk to me, if you really want a relationship with me!" She got near me and gave me a hug and held me tight and for a while I did not move. Then I put my arms around her.

"All right Audrey, I will think of what you said!"

As she left, my mind was confused and felt sad and disappointed. Or maybe I did not want to be challenged out of my comfort zone. I knew I was burying myself in my work, hiding and running away from a broken heart and challenges, also being in an environment where I knew what to do and felt secure.

But at the same time I did love my work and my years passed getting deeper into my work and made my career a path, a way of living, putting everything else aside.

She was challenging me to stretch and I was not sure how I would do it, but really wanted to be with her and to be there for her.

A sparkle of love started to rebirth in my heart and I was maybe afraid to walk or to be bold enough to challenge it and fly with it. The fear of the broken heart and disappointment and being in square one again, walking alone, was something I was not wishing for. But don't we all change, grow, improve and become better people when we are challenged and go through difficulties. We might not always like it but it stretches us and brings out of us strengths, ideas, gifts, abilities that we never thought we had. And we rise to a level that brings us closer to God and puts us on the right path laid in front of us.

Chapter 4
Further away

Was Tuesday morning and Anthony took me back to work and was at a very important meeting. Everyone was expecting me. Of course they were, I was one of the senior partners and had pretty good ideas. It took me time to get used to being called senior partner and the responsibilities to change a bit, but I loved being part of a leadership team and the company was flourishing.

However after the conversation with Audrey I felt hurt and confused and maybe I was fighting the truth that was spoken to me by the Lord through her.

Deep down in my heart I knew she was right, I was in a career and too much connected in my own solicitor mode and my work was first. How would I be able to make time for a relationship in my life? It was impossible at this point. I wanted everything to fit my schedule and my time table, around my work, in my life. Everything was how I wanted.

Self centred, maybe or too much in my own world and did not want to move as a statue.

The days passed and I could not message Audrey, in a way you thought I forgot about her. In a way I did or I was wrestling to forget her. And then on Sundays I would go to church. For some reason, I started to go each Sunday and managed to listen to the service, which I never did before.

The words of the Lord would sink in my heart and slowly do transformation and work his lovely perfect will in my heart.

A different attitude of surrendering to the Lord, taking each day at a time, was getting formed in my heart. I decided that for now, it was better not to think of some things, just pray and just keep going. But I was quite lonely for sure and sad sometimes.

And yes, I would see Audrey at church. She would smile at me, but she never dared to approach me or say anything to me, like we never spoke before and like we never had a few fantastic dinners, walks.

And when you think how well we connected and how amazing we were together. My thoughts were going again at her. She was lovely with her smile, pretty eyes and lovely figure. She did dare to speak the truth to me, but I was too stubborn in my own world.

Another week passed and I did not text her. I could not text her. But she was Sunday in Church. I actually started to look forward to going to church and to being there. Being there and listening to what the Scripture had to say brought me peace and joy. I felt healing in my heart, as my mum already told me.

I could let go of the past.

As the service started with worship I felt connected with the Lord and forgot about everything. Probably was the first time that happened in a long time as my mind was always thinking and planning, organising and was leading on a go go. But this time, my mind was at peace and at rest, it was on a healing journey, resting journey and had an amazing time.

Then the lesson spoke to my heart. Was beautiful and felt the Lord was making a way into my heart: Jeremiah 29:11. The plans the Lord had for me were for good. I felt in my heart that I wanted to do more than work and work, work again. Wanted to experiment more with life and see more, do more. Felt like new air in my lungs and a new beginning.

After the service I enjoyed chatting with some friends I made, lately I chatted with Chris, a new friend I made.

Turning around I just bumped into a lady and she dropped her papers. For a moment I thought it was Audrey but realised it was not her. Said apologises and kept going.

My heart was a bit stressed. Once home I called Dennis. I decided to visit him. He was going to a little church with his wife and since I started going regularly with my mum at church he felt very happy for me. Also I wanted to talk to him about Adurey as I felt so confused. It was time for me to decide what to do and maybe I needed a bit of advice. He was married and probably had a better idea about women than me.

I never probably had that problem before but this time I did and thought it would be better to somehow figure out my next move as I felt frozen and stuck.

As I drove there I felt that I did not want to meet Dennis. However when I knocked at the front door my courage came back and I was ready to talk to Dennis:

"Hey my dear friend! How are you?"

I smiled and entered and he shared with me that Lucy was not home so it was just two of us. I actually was happy and glad that there were two of us.

"I am busy. You know me by now, with my work all the time. My leg is back to normal, so I am back to my life. How are you, Dennis?"

"We are fine, thank you. Lucy cut down a bit the hours as she helps her mother. But it is fine. I earn pretty well and got a raise at work. God is good."

He made a cup of tea and we went into the lounge. We sat down on his comfortable couches.

"How are things with you and Audrey?" he hit the subject I wanted and the reason why I was there.

We chatted a bit and shared a bit about church, Audrey, my mum, usual things, which he knew so well. I guess I was trying to warm up the atmosphere or not sure how to get to the point.

Than I stood up and walked around in the little lounge and then I suddenly turned and looked at him:

"Don't really know Dennis. Can't text her. She does not want to be with me. I would have liked to date her. She wants to date guys that go at church, and said that I need to sort out my life, heart and I work too much, things like this and so on!"

As I kept speaking I got more and more anxious and Dennis told me gently:

"Sit down, Jason!"

I did and was so quiet looking at him and waiting:

"Honestly, Dennis, I don't know what to think and do?" I was looking desperately at him like he would have the right answer and the solution for me.

He looked at me and then he put his head down like in a no.

"I think she was right!"

Shocked, I jumped up!

"What do you mean, Dennis?"

Then I calmed myself and sat down. Looking at me friend I asked again:

"Was she? What do you mean, enlighten me?" I was actually curious.

My friend explained to me and seemed to make sense what he said more than what Audrey said:

"She is a lovely lady that loves the Lord and she does not want to be in the way of your busy life and career. She probably does not feel she has a place in your life at the moment and much more she would like the man she is dating to be going to church like she does. Jason, probably she had a broken heart before and wants someone to be there for her. She is guarding her heart. Look at you, Jason? You are a solicitor and a successful one. You work a lot. When will you have time to date her? Probably she feels she is not up to your standards as well. You see there are a lot of if and if and if. Maybe it makes sense for you. Sometimes my friend, we take it hard to hear some things from the people we care deeply about and it is much easier to hear from an outsider in a way, or a friend. "

Suddenly it all started to make sense to me. Deep down in my heart I knew the truth but was not ready for it, but today I was. I asked my friend hopeless:

"What shall I do? Is there any hope?"

Dennis put his hand on mine:

"What do you want? I know you Jason, for many years you just worked like crazy and I never saw you interested in a woman before. You could have dated lots of successful women and all kinds! But you seem to have a heart that is untouchable. What does your heart want?"

"I would like to date her!"

Then I stood up and walked toward the window and looked at the passers by on the streets and turned toward my friend with a simple smile and a kind voice:

"But it seems too complicated and impossible!"

Sadness was in my heart and my mind, felt hopelessness.

Dennis walked by me and put his hand on my shoulder:

"Jason, the Lord is working in your heart. You will either follow His lead and your life will be changed step by step or either you will keep going on your own path, which I can see did not bring you much joy, even if you are so successful. And probably

Audrey will be one of those new paths opened by the Lord."

We finished chatting about all kinds of sports news and I felt good about visiting my friend.

I was not in the mood to stay late to Dennis and decided to walk back as he was not living far from me.

Started to get dark and cold. I seemed lost in my thoughts.

As I walked back I passed the house of Audrey's nana but I was so caught up in my own thoughts that I did not notice Audrey actually walking toward me.

"Hello Jason!" she said it twice and then out of a dream I stopped, turned my head. But my mind was not there, I hardly noticed her.

"Hello Audrey!"

My heart was sad and was not in the mood for anything. I wanted to be by myself. I was thinking about my life and the path I was on and trying to figure out in which direction my life was going.

"Are you alright Jason??"

"Fine, thank you!"

We both got quiet and we kept looking at each other.

"Have a nice evening Audrey!" I turned around and started to walk.

She whispered as I started walking slowly back to my home:

"I would have liked to hear from you!"

I kept walking as it was a quiet evening. I really enjoyed the walk. Her words did speak to me but

I was in my own castle. What Dennis said was really heavy on my heart as it was the truth and had a lot to think about, pray!

Did not know how I would really move on and what the Lord would expect from me!

There were questions coming and going, what should I do, how should I do it, where was I wrong? How could I improve? What was the Lord expecting from me? What was the next step?

"You are in my prayers Jason!" were Audrey's last words and I did not stop walking and kept going.

When I was home, I went straight to my bedroom. I felt so broken and felt so incapable of doing anything. Told my mum I am tired and want to go to bed early.

No, I did not feel hungry, just felt I wanted to sleep. Felt cold and lonely. Curled under the covers and in no time, I slept like a baby but woke up rested. It felt like it was a new day.

And it was a new day. I had to go to work, and that was all right for me.

Deep down in my heart I took the decision to follow the Lord, the new journey and over the night I prayed and gave my heart to the Lord.

Never done that before, never asked the Lord to come in my heart, to save me, to love me, to help me, never asked for forgiveness and his Spirit!

My thoughts were how to move forward with my life?

I decided to take a step and move. Then the Lord will lead me, so I took the step.

As I went to work, I had a very good morning and felt pretty good, refreshed and joyful.

It was lunch break and I thought of Audrey. Without thinking twice took my phone and just texted her without hesitation or overthinking:

"Hello Audrey, I have been thinking and praying for you too. How are you? Jason"

To my surprise she answered a few minutes later and I was not sure how to react. I felt a joy in my heart and by the end of the work day I sent her another message:

"Would you like to go out for dinner?"

IT was almost 5 pm and I decided not to work late as I used to, just finish work at 5. I tried that before but never managed to do it. I was really determined to have a new beginning and new life, a new start. It felt a bit anxious but exciting and a new journey for me. But I was willing to try and not to give up. Around 6 pm I received a very late message and by then I even forgot I sent her a message:

"Yes, I would love to meet you for dinner?"

"Tomorrow night?"

Sadly the text came back:

"Saturday evening would be great!"

I felt it was better than nothing and wanted to re-organise myself.

Well, it was a new beginning and I was not sure what I was doing. All this week I managed to finish at 5 pm, to be on time home and even my mum was shocked.

No more early mornings like 8 am, I would just start work from 9 am as everyone else and no more weekends working at home. And still finished my entire work. It was amazing to me.

For sure only the Lord was doing that, as I would never have been able to do that before.

All seemed to be something new for me and I even managed to have some sleep. Slowly a desire to know more about Jesus was re-birthing in my heart and I was dedicating a lot of time reading the Bible, spending time with the Lord. I would enjoy my morning praying time before being on my go go day, but also evening time when I would pray and meditate on the Word of God. I felt burdens lifted up from my shoulders and I started to ask my mum lots of questions, even to ask her to pray with me.

My life started in a new direction even if I did not realise slowly the Lord was doing his work in my heart and was working a new path in the wilderness.

That's why he was working slowly and step by step. To reveal to me all his plans would have been too much for me and too scary, That's why the Lord leads step by step.

I was counting in a way the days to meet Audrey but deep down in my heart at the same time was a hidden desire and prayer that I would become the right man for her and she would date me.

IT was amazing how the Lord started to work in my mind and heart. It was a renewal of mind and my heart was slowly transformed, healed!

It was evening and finally we met. We went to a little restaurant for a meal and spent time together.

IT was beautiful and I really enjoyed the weather and it was a great evening. We talked about maybe having a little walk if it was not too cold.

I was ready to meet her and I had no sadness in my heart.

No, we did not meet for some time and I was not sure how she would react when she would see me again. I was not sure how I would react to seeing her again.

We sat quietly at a table and I was a bit hesitant to start the conversation and we started talking about my mum and her friends, then her nan. Slowly the atmosphere started to warm up and we were both smiling.

I stretched my hand over the table and touched hers:

"I really missed you Audrey.!"

She looked at me and unexpectedly said:

"I missed talking to you too, Jason!"

I smiled and then added with a calm voice:

"You were right, I worked too much and lived in a world of my own, and in the past few weeks I started to reconsider my work schedule and everything else and really like it. Also I am having a day off in the middle of the week, Wednesday occasionally. It also seems like a pretty good decision to follow the Lord and my life is slowly moving in a new direction, but I am not sure how, I am taking a day at a time."

She had sparkles in her eyes:

"That is very good Jason, I am so happy for you!"

"What about you?"

I smiled and was waiting for her to tell me some stories from church or something, but Audrey said out of blue:

"I am going south. An aunt, a very far away relative, left me an inheritance and I am going to sort out the house!"

"Oh, that is good. When are you going?"

"Actually I took a week off from work and will try to sort out things and yes… leaving tomorrow!"

That was quite unexpected for me and I did not know how to react. I looked at her and the time seemed to stop for a while. She was so beautiful and she was here with me. I felt so close to her. But at the same time I felt so far away and wished she would have been near me. Maybe my heart was slowly getting connected to this beautiful lovely lady and wanted her to feel the same as me. Sadly I did not feel I really wanted to ask her if she had the same feelings as I started to rebirth for her and was really afraid to ask her. Especially after the conversation we had at my house a few weeks before.

"So, you are going tomorrow. And when are you back?"

"Hope to be back in a week as I have to work. Probably I might need to go again a few times, not sure really, might know more once I am there."

The time passed so quickly and we had quite a lovely time and enjoyed being with each other.

I put no pressure on her about meeting again or about dating. But deep down in my heart was a little sadness and deep desire as I really wanted to date her.

As we were leaving she asked to have a little walk.

And we did have a little walk as it was a bit windy. She was near her car and I did not know how to react and how to say goodbye to her:

"Thank you for a lovely time Audrey."

Was quiet for a moment and our eyes met. She got shy and said:

"Thank you!"

As I was ready to turn around to leave she came slowly near me and she gave me a hug and put her hand around mine gently.

Our hands touched and I took her by hand and held her little hand into mine.

I put my other hand around her and gave her a hug and held her tightly.

"I will miss you!" I took a deep breath.

After few moments I heard a whisper back:

"I will miss you too!"

As she left she added:

"My turn to take you out when I am back, Jason?"

A sparkle was in my heart and joy came back out of blue:

"Yes, Audrey, I would love us to meet again."

Chapter 5
What shall I do?

The week to come passed quite quickly and I was wondering how Audrey was. We did have a few messages during the week but I had not been so brave to suggest a video call. I was not even brave enough to call her. Probably I was slowing down in real life but not in my heart and the way I felt about her. I really thought she was a lovely lady and really missed her.

My busy and successful life started to get lonely and since I met her she made me smile. She brought purpose and a light into my heart. Seemed like my heart was buried into sand deep down as a treasure that was waiting to be discovered.

I felt so lonely without her and till she came into my life I did not realise how lonely I was, or probably I got used to the loneliness and living my own way of life burying myself in work, surrendering myself with friends that I did not need or they actually did not need me.

Everything was so busy and complicated for me. You could say I was doing all the right things career wise but not regarding family life. Majority of my colleagues at work were married or had someone. I was one of the ones that was never interested in anyone. The "lonely wolf". All till Audrey. I actually gave up more than ten years even searching for someone and if I ever was invited to a party I was just polite. My friends would keep introducing me to all kinds of lovely ladies but none brought sparkles into my heart or desire or passion, nothing at all.

Love was quite far away for me, or impossible!

After a while I guess my friends kind of gave up on me and the years passed so quickly.

On the Sunday when I was expecting Audrey to come back, I received a message from her:

"Hi Jason! I am coming back home this evening. Maybe we can meet in the week for a drink if you want or dinner?"

I loved the way she was so simple and direct, so sweet at the same time. Seemed a long time to wait for her and I was ready for it. My heart was yearning to see her again.

Of course I accepted the invitation and each day I counted till I was going to see her. That day came and it was quite an unexpected day.

Yes, we met, yes we went for dinner. All seemed too good, too lovely and flowing. I was not sure what to think, but felt a bit like something was going to happen and I was not sure what it was. When she just said out of the blue:

"Jason, I inherited a beautiful property and I had been considering moving there. Seems a very quiet area and I could easily find a job as a nurse as it is a small hospital in the neighbourhood." and she waited for my reaction.

Trying to smile, I was trying to hide the struck in my heart and pain that I felt but maybe I was not doing such a good job after all.

"So, you might not come back here, again."

Audrey looked at me a bit confused and wondering:

"Not sure yet what the Lord wants me to do, but thought I would like to share with you. So, you can pray for me, please."

"Of course I will. The Lord will direct your steps, I am sure." they were the only words that I could say to her.

"Thank you!" she wanted to say something else but she did not. She seemed to have changed her mind or was hesitant in her behaviour with me.

The rest of the evening felt quite quiet and sad in a way.

My heart got locked back in its own little castle and I was in my own thoughts. I used to do that many times when I was hurt or sad. My mum knew that and she used to leave me alone, but probably no one else did know how I was.

Home as soon as I arrived, I wanted to have a chat with the Lord. Seemed to be the best idea lately and really enjoyed having new revelation, insight into many things, and some I never thought before. The wisdom of the Lord was getting deeper and deeper for me, I was thirsty for it.

Well, it was Friday evening and tomorrow was Saturday and I had no plans.

"Here is me, Jason. Lord. Yes, me again. Yes, now I want to talk, I have so many questions and I just don't know what to do. I would like you to help me and direct me, I need help with everything. Well, Audrey is leaving, Lord. Or maybe not? I really don't know what I should do or not do."

I started to move quickly around my room from window to door and from door to window. I was so anxious. I put my hand on my heart and realised it was hurting me.

"No, Lord, I do not want her to leave. I do not want that. You know how I feel, I can not hide that from you. You know my heart, Lord."

I heard a knock at the door and my mum asked with her gentle voice:

"Are you alright in there? You seem to fall down through the ceiling!"

"Come in mum" I looked at the door as she entered.

She sat near me and probably I was looking very gloomy as she kissed me on the cheek.

"What's wrong, Jason?"

For a moment I nodded and did not feel like talking.

"Audrey, she wants to move down south...."

My mum looked at me and with her soft voice said:

"You really like her a lot!"

I stood up upset:

"Of course I do, I am in love with her."

My mum made a sign for me to sit down near her:

"Did you tell her how you feel? Did you speak with her?"

She always knew how to reach my heart and bring me to the point of tension or the matter.

"No, I did not!"

"Why not, Jason?"

I knew where she was going and it was so hard for me, but the Lord was getting to my heart, He was teaching me:

"Because, because I can not. Probably she will say no."

And my face looked confused, touched my heart with my hand and nodded my head.

My mum gave me a hug. She was always such a lovely lady and even when my father treated me and Paul badly, she always stood up for me.

I smiled sad and said:

"Thank you mum."

As she left she added with a kind voice looking at me:

"Don't give up. Go and talk to her! There is still hope!"

The night passed and like this Saturday I just went for a walk and then spent the afternoon home, watching Netflix.

Sunday at church, I did see Audrey and my mum looked at me wondering, but I did not move. Could not, even if I wanted to.

In my heart I wanted to move and talk to her and tell her how I felt and that I did not want her to leave, but in reality, I did absolutely nothing. I was not ready and I was not ready, that was it.

The days passed very quickly and sadness came back into my heart and loneliness. I felt that my job was a distraction in a way, that the days were so long. I even stopped texting Audrey.

And than suddenly when less expected I received a message saying:

"Hi, Jason! How are you? I had been texting you a few messages and was wondering if you got them or you might have changed your number and I am texting somebody else!"?

This time I wanted to text her and replied:

"Hi Audrey, thank you for your messages. So sorry for not answering, but I was very busy. Would you like to meet, if you are still in town as I need to talk to you?"

For few hours no answer and then late afternoon I received a message:

"Yes, Jason, we can meet tomorrow, it is Friday again and I am not working this weekend."

Friday evening came and I was ready to meet her. Had two scenarios in mind: To tell her or not to tell her. Not quite much of a plan but was a start.

As I was waiting for her in our little Italian restaurant, It crossed my mind to stand up and leave. The tension was a bit too much for me and maybe I should move on, leave and just forget it.

But something made me stay still and I was still waiting for Audrey. When she came I stood up, she looked amazing. Her beautiful eyes and smile captivated me from the first time and was still captivating me. I felt a sparkle in my heart. Even if she was dressed in a pair of jeans with a red blouse and a jumper she looked so beautiful.

I smiled and felt at the same time anxious but also excited to see her.

"Hi Audrey, you look so beautiful!"

Got near her and gave her a gentle kiss on the cheek.

She got shy and smiled at me:

"Hi Jason, you always compliment me. Thank you."

We ordered the food, drinks and were talking about my boring work:

"You know, solicitors are not always loved, especially when the bill hits." I laughed.

"Well, nurses are always chasing and let's say it, we are always on a go go and deal with sick people. Was wondering what is worse: sick or broke or maybe it is both. As we deal with broken people in pain." she laughed.

We got quiet for a moment and Audrey looked at me:

"What are you thinking, Jason?"

"Not sure if it is best for me to share?"

She looked at me and touched my hand and out of instinct I took her hand into mine.

"All right, I will, everything or nothing. What can I lose? Hey!"

Audrey looked at me and seemed confused:

"I do not understand!"

I was actually speaking to myself and getting my courage I looked into her eyes and spoke:

"Audrey, I love your company, you are beautiful, intelligent, fun to be around and I fell in love with you. I would like to date you and go out with you. I had been a "lonely wolf" for years, buried in my career and you brought love in my heart. I just want to be with you. However you already said lots of things to me a few weeks ago and now you also want to move and don't want to lose you. But I had to tell you how I feel. I am not perfect, it is true, but I am trying my best, Audrey! Can you give me a chance?"

Could not look at her and for a moment, felt tired and ashamed but relieved that I told her.

"Jason!" she started.

"Aww, that is beautiful what you said, and I believe you are an amazing man, but I will need to think of what you said. I can not give you an answer now. As you know I did consider moving south as well."

Our eyes met and for a moment I felt she did care about me, but maybe I was just imagining and did not say anything regarding the love subject for the rest of the evening. I enjoyed every bit of her company and we had an amazing time.

The evening finished pretty quick in a way and I was back in my lonely room.

My heart felt free as I did share with her and told her how I felt. Now I just had to wait. Was just praying and waiting. Trusting the Lord was something unknown to me as I was not the best at waiting and always did things my own way. Walking step by step with the Lord, trusting him as he was guiding me it was a new road that I was learning slowly. Enjoying bit by bit, day by day and taking a day at a time was in a way new for me. It was like an adventure.

My mum as well as my colleagues at work said I changed. I did not think I did, only felt challenged and stretched to the limit with patience. I started to enjoy my structured program at work and had more time to myself on the weekends.

I used to paint long ago and it was an interesting hobby that I have not done in a long time.

But I decided to restart doing it. I was told I had been pretty good but did not care about compliments, I enjoyed painting and it was relaxing to me. In a way, it was a very unusual hobby for me.

Probably I enjoyed painting as it was quiet and also was something that was directing my mind from buzzing all the time with decisions and things that were challenging me.

When I was painting I was in my own world and loved it.

Chapter 6
Wrestling with God

That evening when I was home, Clara came and sat near me on the couch as I was cuddling the cat and was quiet.

"Audrey, is everything all right?"

I always enjoyed talking with Clara. She was tall and quiet with a lovely personality and seemed to bring peace and calm with her voice. They were so unique and lovely, both sisters Lucy and Clara. Lucy was the one that brought joy to my heart and made me feel bouncy in a way and giggle. Two sisters with such a complex personality were both my aunties and they were looking after me like I was their daughter. They offered me over years more love and prayer and support than anyone else in my life. I was very fond of them, I loved them and were for me my family.

"Yes, I think so. I am determined to move, you know Clara."

"Yes, I understand you want a change and we both, myself and Lucy, respect that. You already showed us pictures with the beautiful house and it is lovely. You could have your own family one day.

Out of the blue she spoke upset:

"No, I will not date him!"

Audrey got up the couch and was agitated. Something deep down in her heart was stirring love. She did not realise it was something that was thinking of more than anything.

At that moment Lucy entered into the lounge and asked surprised:

"Who are you not dating?"

Audrey got red and purple, pink in her face and could not avoid the subject. Even if she wanted to hid the things for few days from her aunties, now for sure she could not:

"Jason. I met Jason tonight, you know that. He asked me to date him and told me that he started to fall in love with me."

"Both aunties were so joyful and Lucy giggled clapping hands:

"Great news, and you said yes!" and she was so happy.

"No, of course. No!" I was so determined.

Audrey sounded almost angry and upset and both aunties were very shocked.

With her calm tactic questions Clara wanted an answer:

"Why did you not answer yes, Audrey? We both know you met quite a few times and you always enjoy his company.

Audrey looked at them. This time she was calm and shared with her aunties:

"Jason is a very good friend, but he is a solicitor with a big career in a different world than mine."

Clara tried to take his side made few points:

"But he does go to church with his mum and he said he is praying for you. He has a job and is successful. What is wrong with that? At least he can pay the bills."

Audrey was quite determined and her mind was not willing to negotiate. Her heart was unmovable, like a rock this time:

"Yes, but he does not have a deep walk with the Lord and he works too much. I have my life. I should not have met him anymore. It is probably my fault."

Lucy giggled and she started to make tea in the kitchen and all followed her.

"Tea and cake?"

"Yes please!" said Lucy.

"No, just some tea, auntie Clara!"

The question that was flying through the air came finally:

"What do you feel about him?"

"Stop pressuring her, Clara. She might not want to tell us that."

"IS ok," made a sign with her hand Audrey.

"I do not know how I feel about him and maybe I am afraid to think of it. Anyway best will be for me to move on, to focus and pray about moving."

"Did you ask the Lord?"

Don't we all do that, avoid or forget and we do not ask the Lord being afraid of the answer, challenge.

"No and yes? About what auntie Clara?"

"Did you ask the Lord about Jason, my dear?"

That was quite something she did not. She did pray for Jason but never asked the Lord for more than a friendship or about his heart.

"Go to the Lord and sit at his feet and listen to his voice. Ask him if you should date Jason or not?"

Surprised of the ideas that were given to me, and the wisdom given by the Lord ot my aunties, I realised the Lord was trying to talk to me and I was not listening:

"Yes, that is true. I should go and seek the Lord, ask him to guide me and answer my prayers. But I am sure the answer will be no."

It was silence for a moment and Clara added:

"Ask the Lord and listen to his answer and follow Him"

That evening as Audrey went to bed she spent time praying and tried to bring everything to the Lord. But each time when she was praying for Jason she felt a sparkle in her heart.

Was something there and did not want to go so deep. Maybe it was not such a good idea after all to pray for Jason and ask about dating or not. He was a dear friend that once she would move would not be able to see him again and she will for sure make new friends.

But was that really what she wanted and was that really what the Lord wanted?

Deep down in her heart she smiled as she thought of Jason and a sparkle was in her eyes. But put her hand at her front and dismissed the thoughts:

"No, I will be moving. No. No. I can not and could not date Jason. She felt she was in a battle. Her heart seemed to want something else and then she spoke boldly:

"If you want Jason to date me you will have to make a way, make a way. Otherwise I am determined to move south and that's it. A few hours' distance is fine. My life will move in a different direction."

"Do you like Jason!" the Lord spoke to her heart.

"Lord, I do not want to think of him, I want to move on!"

I dismissed and carried on praying for all my family, friends and left Jason last, but did not pray for dating him.

I focussed my prayers on what I wanted and felt confident about moving and having a different future.

In a way I was running away from Jason and avoiding looking into my heart. I could not deal with certain things. I was not ready.

My aunties did not bring Jason into conversation, but by their silence I knew they were praying and they did not agree with me even if they did not share yet their opinions fully.

***

After a week of silence in the house I decided to talk to them:

"Why are you quiet with me regarding Jason? I want to know what you think?"

Clara smiled as she was knitting on the armchair:

"You do not want our opinion and need it. You already made up your mind and decided your life path. What do you want to know, it does not matter, does it?"

Lucy was as usual moving around as she liked cooking and cleaning. They were only working 3 days a week and kind of home helping and looking after me. Lucy taught me a lot of cooking recipes and Clara was pretty good at teaching me about plants and loved doing gardening with my aunties.

"So, what is your view?"

"Date him. You are meant for eachother!" Lucy giggled and I was so shocked that I thought I would fall down from the couch!

And immediately changed the subject.

I already made plans to move in a couple of months and did not resign yet from my work but I was about to do it as well, was in my plans but kept delaying it.

Deep down in my heart I was trying to avoid Jason and stopped texting him for a week. Then decided to text him again, but my heart was so excited and felt I wanted to meet him and was thinking of him quite a lot.

"Hi Jason. Thank you for everything. Hope will meet again for a drink. Just wanted to let you know that I decided to go south and will be moving soon. Wish you all the best and blessings. Audrey."

Sounded so cold, so far away, not actually deep as our friendship. Well, it had to be done.

Had to be done, I kept telling myself that I made the best decision in moving. Or I was trying to convince myself or run away.

I was so determined to move that my aunties did not say anything anymore and felt quite sad.

But deep down in my heart was Jason. Buried there was Jason.

What I thought of him was a forbidden subject.

One day as I was visiting my nana, unexpectedly I saw him passing by and was hoping he would not see me. I forgot he was doing his walks and was passing by my nana's house many times.

He stopped and that moment my heart went racing as speedy:

"Hi Audrey, how are you?"

Not sure what to expect, he seemed to treat me with distance.

"Hi Jason. How are you?"

"I am fine, busy and working. I am back to my old hobby: my painting."

After a moment of silence, both of us were more or less looking in other directions being embarrassed:

"I've understood from your text that you are moving south. I wish you all the best Audrey."

For a moment Audrey did not react and Jason approached her and with slow movements gave her a hug and held her tight in his arms:

"Audrey, tell me what do you think of me and feel for me?" added those beautiful words looking into her eyes.

She backed down slowly and looked at him surprised:

"We are just ….! It does not matter, not anymore, Jason."

I looked at her and smiled:

"You know Audrey, someone told me long ago and did not understand it only 10 years down the line, recently: You are wrestling with the Lord! And at that point I did not understand it. But if I would have, I would not have wasted 10 years. Now I understand. Audrey, you are wrestling with the Lord. I will miss you, however you made your choice."

"Yes, Jason. All the best" and she turned around and left as it was too much for her to bear with it.

And that was her battle and she had to be broken and her eyes open but she was wrestling and deep down she knew that.

But not now, now was not the time for her to admit.

Her prayers were of what she thought would be best and she did not listen to the Spirit and she was not willing to. Her test ended up in an open door that she wanted to go and leave everything behind.

Was she running away from Jason, herself, future, trust, pain. Yes she was. But she was not at the point of admitting her own faults and her own weaknesses, that was quite far off for her.

A new life was waiting for her and she was looking forward to it. In a way was running away from herself, her feelings, being afraid she would be hurt again and end up alone.

Chapter 7
My Mum went to heaven

It was raining and cold and I was alone. I opened the main door and wished for my mum to call me. But she did not. She was not here anymore. She went to heaven to be with the Lord.

How did it all happen?

Audrey left and a month passed and I was alone. Back on the same road praying so much for the Lord would not to take her away, but she still left, moved and stopped texting me.

I tried to move on but I could not. I kind of buried myself again as I did before, except at that time, I already accepted the Lord in my heart and was even baptised in the church. Everything was new for me and my mum was so happy. But one day coming back from work. Everything changed when I found my mum.

She was laying on the floor and she was barely breathing. I called the ambulance. My beautiful mum, how could I leave her? She just whispered to me:

"Stay close to the Lord and don't let go of Audrey! Find her."

She was smiling, even if she was hardly breathing. The doctor did warn her about a second heart attack but she was not afraid. She kept going, probably I used to follow her as an example.

"I love you, Jason! Stay close to the Lord! You look after yourself!" And then closed her eyes. A few minutes later the ambulance came.

When we arrived at the hospital, there was not much hope. She went to be with the Lord a few minutes after arriving, in spite of all the effort to bring her back. My eyes were invaded with tears and so much pain that my heart could not bear.

Could not remember how long I waited at the hospital till my friend Dennis came and took me home. I was there for a couple of hours. Just staring in the waiting room.

The Lord was with me and brought me comfort, but really missed my mum. She really brought joy to me and could not imagine my life without her. Was so lonely.

My days were really lonely and I kept thinking of Audrey. I was missing her so much. I wished she would have been here. But she was not. I wished my life would not take this path at this moment but there was and was nothing I could do about it.

My heart sank, she was not with me anymore.

And now after 2 weeks this house seems big for me and so cold and I wished I would live somewhere else. I could afford it.

I was thinking of selling the house.

Another month and my life was on the move and I did move into a new house. Was a 3 bedroom house and was in a quiet lovely neighbourhood and I loved it. Made me feel it was a new beginning for me and deep down in my heart I needed that.

My thoughts were not much anymore at Audrey, but I was still praying for her. But in a way I stopped praying to date her. She moved on with her life and she was in her own world and she made her own choice, I was in mine. I did not agree with her choice but I respected her.

In a way that was a No to dating me even if she never said it.

What was the point of me really asking her for a date? I never understood at that point but the Lord would reveal that to me at a later stage when all the pieces of the puzzle will be together.

The words of my mum to go and search for Audrey were still resounding in my heart and mind, however I felt I should not go and search for Adurey. What was the point? I already asked for a date long ago and she said no by telling me she is moving away.

That was enough for me and it did not make sense what else I could tell her or how I would convince her.

Probably was better just to carry on with my life and did not want to have again the bitter painful taste of love unfulfilled as I started having feelings for Audrey!

After few more weeks, I received a message:

"Hi Jason, I am visiting the town and was thinking if you would like to go out for dinner? Audrey"

That was not something I was considering anymore, but when I saw her name, a sparkle was led again in my heart. I decided to pray and sleep over it. I have not really decided what to do: yes or no!

Was something that I was not really considering!

Sunday came and went at church. I really enjoyed the service and made lots of new friends and was looking forward to having a chat with them.

In the middle of the worship, someone sat next to me and when I turned around to just say hello, I was very shocked to see it was Audrey. She was sitting next to me in church.

My mind stopped and had no words. My heart started to wrestle and I felt quite anxious. Feelings buried deep down started invading my heart and in no way I could stop them.

I did enjoy the preaching and everything and did not speak with Audrey till everything was over.

She smiled and asked me politely how I was and then she was ready to leave as I did not have much conversation.

My heart felt prompted by the Lord and I called her:

"Audrey, shall we meet at 4 pm?"

She smiled and nodded a yes and added:

"I would love that!"

What a day for me, I wasn't even sure why I was meeting her, maybe to catch up. Maybe hoping, but deep down I knew I missed her and still wanted to be with her.

That afternoon came and I had mixed feelings from being anxious to really wanting to see her. But maybe it was not right as my heart was still in love with her and she moved away. I really did not want my heart broken, but probably was in a way as she left.

We were sitting in front of each other and we were both quiet and just smiling.

"Audrey, how is it there? Do you like it?"

"Yes, it is a lovely quiet town with lovely people, a very nice area!"

I was quite well behaved and did not touch her hand or anything with initiative like that. I understood she just wanted to be friends and respected her.

She looked into my eyes and knew she would ask about my mum:

"I've heard about your mum, I am really sorry, she was a lovely lady and always there for everyone."

"Yes, things have changed since she went to be with the Lord. I sold the house and live now in a three bedroom property not far away from where we lived before. She was everything to me and always there, very good loving mum. I miss her a lot."

My eyes got sad and was not sure what I was doing here and wanted to talk more than hi and goodbye and simple subjects with Audrey, we used to go deep into debates and opinions and loved being with her. But tonight I felt the battle was not mine and that I did all my best. I was just here. It was up to her.

We finished the main meal and Audrey showed signs of anxiety. She apologised and said she would like to go home.

I drove her home as it started to rain and be cold. It was spring and a beautiful March but it rained today.

"Thank you Audrey, it was nice to see you and I wish you all the best and blessings in your new life adventure in another part of the country. Hope all works well for you."

Was quiet and she did not say anything.

She was still beautiful and I felt sad to say goodbye to her.

I turned my head toward her and she just looked at me as a sight came out of her heart:

"Ohh, Jason!" and she touched my face with her hand gently, looking for a moment deep into my eyes:

"I really missed you!" was more like a whisper and before I realised what happened she was out of the car and in the house.

Smiling sad, I drove off and was ready to get into my bed. I loved spending time with the Lord, quiet time and it was very quiet since my mum was not around.

I really missed her and it seemed to me that the Lord was carrying me through a new season, helping me and supporting me and reshaping me. My life was redirected in a different direction.

Tomorrow was Saturday and had nothing planned, probably late lay in, read and then paint, then watch some TV and read and have a very quiet evening. It was just me and my best friend, a cat called Kathy.

****

As Audrey entered the doors she sat straight down on the couch and covered her face with her hands and started to cry.

"Oh my, oh my goodness. What is wrong?" Lucy got agitated.

Then calling for other sister:

"Clara, Clara, come down, our little girl is sad!"

Lucy put her arms around Audrey giving her a cuddle and asked her gently:

"What is wrong, Audrey!?"

Clara came down but she was more gentle with questions and very calm:

"Audrey, if you want us to leave you alone we can, but you do know we worry for you and we want you to be happy. Did someone upset you?"

Through tears she looked at them and she said with a deep breath:

"I missed him so much!"

Both of them got a bit confused:

"Missed who?"

"Jason, of course. Who else? I met him today and just realised how much I missed him. But it doesn't matter anymore as I am trying to establish myself somewhere else. And probably he does not want to date me anymore."

As Adurey was calming herself down and Lucy made a cup of tea, Clara as she always had ideas added:

"Lets pray and see what the Lord will work: Dear Lord we ask for wisdom and revelation of your will, for you to work your grace and mercy. Reveal to us what shall we do regarding Audrey and Jason. We do not know and we do not understand some things, but Audrey is very upset and hurt. We bring those two lovely people in front of you so you, the mighty God will make a way to their hearts and bring your will to pass. In the mighty name of Jesus we pray. Amen!"

It was silence for few minutes then Clara asked:

"What are your heart desires, Audrey?"

Looking at her aunt she smiled:

"My heart was very much confused and unsure. But tonight as I met Jason, I realised that I really missed him so much. I did enjoy his company, however now my life seems to move to a different part of the country and I won't be able to meet him. We are just friends. And nothing more will ever be between us. We will fade in time."

"Would you like to date him?"

It was total quietness. She did not say anything and was rubbing her hands agitated.

"Well, Audrey, you need to be honest with the Lord and yourself. The truth does set you free!"

"Yes, sooner or later I need to be honest with the Lord and with myself."

"So what is the truth, Audrey?"

Looking a bit worried and a bit meditating she decided to be open and truthful to herself:

"I do enjoy Jason and he is fun to be with, very intelligent and a gentleman and very handsome. We have very good deep conversations, we laugh and also he started to draw near to the Lord. He is so much like me in a way and so different. That's all."

"And? "

Confused she looked at Clara:

"Would you like to date him or not?"

"No, no! We are just friends."

Then after a few minutes of silence she spoke almost shouting:

"Of course I would love to be with him, he is amazing!"

Both sisters more shocked looked at her and laughed the same time:

"What are you waiting for girl, send him a text."

Few minutes past 9 I received a message:

"Hi Jason, Thank you for tonight. Was lovely to see you!

I know that is short notice and probably you have other plans, but can we meet tomorrow maybe at the park and maybe dinner at 5 pm? IF not is ok, I understand. But please let me know when you are free? Would really love to talk with you about a few very important things that are on my heart. Audrey"

As nothing planned for tomorrow I was pondering what to do and the Lord prompted me to accept. So I accepted her invitation and was looking forward to meeting her to really find out what it was about.

Chapter 8
Shall I be with you?

It was a sunny day and the rain left a refreshed atmosphere and the beautiful colourful spring flowers were making the park look so pretty and friendly. Lots of people were walking, strolling through the park and me too. I was meeting Audrey at our place near a fountain and I was eager to see what it was about. Seemed very important and I did not want to be late.

Also deep down in my heart I was taking advantage to see her again, probably for the last time before she was returning this week back to her new house and life, far far away.

As soon as I saw her, I waved. And she came near me and I leaned toward her and gave her a kiss on the cheek. It was something that I was not planning, but I wanted to be near her.

She turned toward me and smiled:

"Thank you Jason for coming."

"You know I like being with you. So what would you like to do Audrey? Would you like to take a walk, or dinner?"

She was so beautiful and she was with me, it did not matter what I was doing as long as she was here with me.

For a moment I was unsure what to do and what to think, but I decided to enjoy the evening and to wait to see if she would bring the matter, whatever she wanted to talk about with me. Probably she needed some advice or prayers for something.

We had a lovely time and we talked about the beautiful season of spring, plants and flowers. We always enjoyed talking deep and she spoke about the Lord and how she was learning new things regarding patience.

It was quiet for a moment and we were all enjoying our dinner. Then she stopped. She put down her fork and knife and looked at me:

"Jason!" She was very serious and I felt that my heart started to race and I was not sure what to think or believe. I was ready for whatever she would gone tell me. Could not be so bad after all.

"I decided to come and speak with you!"

"Yes, I am listening. Whatever I can help with, I will try my best."

I seemed very interested and I was all here for her:

"You know that for the past few weeks I was going and coming to look after my late aunt's property and was praying to see what the Lord wants me to do."

She was waiting for me to confirm and to make sure in a way I understood her. So far I did but was not sure where she was going with that.

"I just realised that I really enjoy your company and would really love to meet you more."

"Of course, when you visit again back here, I would love that." I agreed with her.

She looked at me and she seemed quite determined and I added trying to be supportive:

"I enjoy being with you, however I know it will be harder as you move away, but if you need my help. Let me know!"

Audrey looked at me and seemed surprised:

"You do not understand Jason."

"Don't I?" I was a bit confused, smiling at the same time.

"Few weeks ago, you asked me for a date."

As I did not want to talk about that subject I interrupted her:

"Yes, I know. Is ok, I understand you moved and have other priorities. I should have not bothered you with that. You obviously had other plans and that was not toward me."

Audrey listened very patient and then she spoke with her kind voice:

"My answer Jason is YES. I would love to go out with you."

For a moment I was like a petrified statue and did not move and could not believe it what I was hearing:

"Are you serious?" and our eyes met.

Audrey stretched her hand and I took it into mine.

"Yes, I am. I got really fond of you and we became good friends. Let's say I started to fall in love with you without planning. I enjoy your company and you get closer to God. I know it is a journey. You have a very good heart and you are a man of integrity."

Whilst she was telling me those things she looked into my eyes and smiled. She waited for my reply.

"Audrey,... I am a bit shocked!"

"If you have somebody else I understand or if you changed your mind. You did ask me more than a month ago I think."

Felt shocked and my heart was invaded of feelings, joy and once I calmed down after couple of minutes I spoke:

"NO, I do not have anyone else and no I did not change my mind. Let me do the right thing: Audrey, would you like to date me?" I smiled and stretched my hand again, over the table to catch hers.

Smiling and shy she nodded and answered:

"Would love to be your girlfriend."

Could not believe it as we had a magical evening and I was walking hand in hand with my beautiful lovely girlfriend.

That was something that I did not plan or expect and felt overwhelmed by God's grace and favour.

Me, the lonely Jason, was having a girlfriend and my world was different. But I was not ready to jump like some of my colleagues bragging that they had a girlfriend or that they bought something or that they are going to have an expensive holiday. I was quite humbled and quiet as a personality but bold and confident when it was about my job. I was probably a very interesting combination and my colleagues really respected me. I've worked hard to earn my respect.

Regarding Audrey, she was a blessing, a deepest desire that came out from the Lord. I was very disappointed and hurt and in a way heart broken when she was telling me she was considering moving. For the past few weeks nothing happened and even our messages had no indication that things were going to move in the right direction; however, the Lord was the one that was searching and working in our hearts, guiding our footsteps.

I wanted to share with someone but I did not, I was not ready.

As I entered my house I went straight upstairs and in a few minutes I was in my bed.

Staring at the ceiling I started to talk with the Lord and could not believe it that Audrey said: Yes!

"Lord, you are full of surprises and your grace and favour overwhelms me. Thank you for Audrey! Your ways are higher than mine and your will is better than mine. The way you work in my heart and put in place each puzzle in my life is amazing and I have not enough words to say thank you and praise you. Not only because you are my Father and Saviour but also because you are God. You are good and you chose to work in our lives and hearts according to your glory and grace. Thank you Lord."

***

My week started pretty well and it was a good beginning and then something happened and from being filled with joy I got sad and confused again. Audrey stopped texting me and I was not sure what was going on. I assumed that she was busy as I knew she was going to sort out the house back in the south.

As we just started dating, I was not sure if she was ready for it or if I was rushing it. Maybe she needed some space and she did have to sort out papers with solicitors and agencies to sell the property.

All of that dating idea was a bit new for me and I was trying to adjust with it. I did not talk to anyone about it, except my Lord.

Felt peace and trust and new open doors for a new part of my life. Some had lovely families, some had lovely careers, some were travelling, some were … Well, everyone had something and I had a career and really wanted a balanced life with family and work.

Since mum died I felt really lonely with my cat and felt really quiet in the house. But the thought of having and being more around Audrey brought a smile on my face and a new purpose for my life.

So like this passed Tuesday and Wednesday and Thursday and no news still and I started to wonder if she changed her mind.

Maybe she decided after all to stay there and I was just left alone in my own world waiting. Yes, thoughts of confusion and worries were going and coming and I was not sure how to deal with them, but started each time to bring them to the Lord.

During the day I was busy at work and it kept my mind out of it, but at home I was thinking what shall I do.

Then I remembered that she had a nan and her two aunties but did not know their phone number.

I was in a very interesting situation and it was already Thursday evening. Friday came as well so quickly and my patience reached the limit.

I really needed to move forward. I prayed and did ask the Lord for answers and somehow to know about her, or what is going on.

Home I was looking forward to the weekend, as was home, and it was Friday evening. Me and my cat were watching a lovely movie on Netflix. Something easy and fun with Jackie Chan that made me laugh and relax.

As I was in the middle of the movie, I heard my phone buzzing and kind of ignored it. I was not in the mood for any work colleagues and for sure not for work messages. I was not working anymore on weekends and that was a new rule, discipline that took me a few months of ups and downs to follow but really worked well.

Was quiet and I was almost asleep. I didn't really mind if I would have fallen asleep on the couch, when my phone started to ring. It really scared me and as I got up, I realised it was 9.30 very late and the movie was still on.

"Hello, this is Jason Wright! How can I help?" I answered politely as I could not recognise the number.

"Hello, Jason. This is Clara Martin. Me and Lucy are Audrey's Jones Aunties. As you know she lives with us. We are sorry to disturb you but we were trying to get a hold on you for the past two days and finally somehow we found your phone number."

"Yes, Audrey spoke a lot of lovely words about you."

I felt a bit intrigued and curious same time and totally awake for sure:

"We received a few days ago a phone call from Mayfield Valley town that Audrey was involved in a car crash and she was in hospital."

That was totally shocking for me and I did not know how to react. I was anxious and eager to hear more.

"IS she all right?"

"Jason, we spoke with the doctor on the phone and he said she is fine and that she will probably be released in a few days. Her leg was injured but otherwise she is fine. We assume she won't be able to work for a while, probably a few weeks."

"Would it be all right if I would get in contact with the hospital?"

Polite and with her calm voice Clara answered:

"You are her boyfriend, I am sure she would love to speak with you."

As concerned as I was, I did not even pray and my mind was racing as quick as my heart and I was ready to talk to her. I wanted to see her. And I picked up the phone and called the number that Clara gave me.

A very polite lady answered and she even offered, if Audrey was not asleep, to let me speak with her.

I honestly forgot about protocol and policies in place and when you are supposed to call and how you are supposed to do it.

"Hello" I heard a weak sleepy voice on the other side.

"Audrey, hello. This is Jason."

"Hello Jason" her voice got a sparkle.

"How are you?"

"So happy you called, I had been thinking of you."

"I've missed you. Just wanted you to know, I had been praying for you and looking forward to seeing you."

I've heard a nurse in the background and Audrey spoke with a sleepy voice:

"I am tired and sleepy. I wish you would be here, Jason."

"I will be there soon."

"Goodnight Jason. So lovely you called." and she hung up the phone, probably very tired.

My weekend plans changed and I organised a little bag for myself with things and was ready to go in the morning. I was determined to drive to Mayfield Valley to see Audrey and be there for her.

I already spoke with the hospital and they were happy for me to visit as I was travelling from far far away.

Spending time with the Lord was best before bed time!

Saturday was the day of going to Mayfield Valley.

The drive there was really good and took me a few hours. But that was ok, I did not mind the drive. I was happy to stop by a Fast food half way through and hope seemed to be back in my heart.

Audrey started to become important to me and I really wanted to take care of her. I was determined to make this relationship work in a way and try to be a good boyfriend however I felt I had no clue many times what I was doing.

As more and more as I was spending time with the Lord I found more and more desire to be into the Word deeper and deeper and going higher and higher into different levels of wisdom and paths of new revelations.

Things that did not make sense started to be in a different light and new ideas, opportunities started to open for past days and that was something interesting to me and really felt the Lord was challenging me to new levels not only by bringing Audrey into my life but also into my career and my new church path.

I was missing my mother but having Audrey was the beginning of something beautiful.

I still was wondering if I was good enough for her and felt a bit of guilt and condemnation which I started to realise was not from the Lord.

I've made a new friend Mike at church and enjoyed going for lunch occasionally. He seemed like a nice young man and his wife Marie was a lovely lady. Mike was my age and was working into a large company and was managing production of different types of furniture.

I was still meeting Dennis and those two became kind of my close friends in a way. So, I decided to ask them to back me up in prayers this time. Was the time for me to get out of my shell in a way. So I messaged my friends. Was good to have lovely good friends to be with you in different paths of your life.

As I parked the car at the hospital I was back to reality and ready to visit with Audrey.

I was not sure if I could bring her flowers, but did and had a lovely bouquet of roses, yellow and red and also a couple of books.

With excitement I asked at the reception and they guided me to floor 3. As I was approaching the unit my heart went crazy and was not sure how to speak with her and what to say to her.

A lady at a small office told me to wait a few minutes.

When she returned she asked me to follow her.

The room where Audrey was was more like a saloon with 3 more people and she was near the window.

She was not asleep and as soon as she saw me she smiled. She looked so beautiful, but a bit pale, but probably I did not notice as I was so focused on her.

"Hey Audrey!" came near her and was not sure what to do and she stretched her hand and came near her and kissed her on the cheek. She was so beautiful and so lovely.

She whispered to me:

"I really missed you!"

Our eyes met and I smiled and took a chair and sat next to her bed.

"How are you? I had been worrying for you!"

She looked pale and tired, but her eyes had that beautiful sparkle:

"Did you, really? Did you think I would leave?"

That moment I looked so serious at her:

"Yes, I did. I thought you changed your mind."

Looking at me she asked for my hand and I held it into mine:

"No, Jason. I do not plan on leaving!"

"Good, because you are the best thing that happened to me and I do not plan to lose you."

At that moment the door opened and a doctor entered and came straight to Audrey's bed. I was not sure what to do, but the doctor made a sign that it is ok and I can stay.

"Good morning Audrey. This is your handsome man, Jason!"

"Yes, he is. And he rushed to come and visit me."

"Nice to meet you young man. I think you are younger than me. I will be fifty five next week. Getting younger within one year. Hey!"

The doctor was joking and in a good mood.

"Now, the good news is Audrey. I can release you today. Only if you want to leave. Otherwise I can keep you till Monday."

My face was shining and felt so good.

"Really!" I seemed quite enthusiastic.

"Yes, her leg is much better" and he pulled the cover a bit and showed me that under the knee, on her left leg was a bandage.

Then carried on explaining.

"All her tests are fine, the only concern was how quick it will heal and make sure it will not get infected."

"Thank you very much for everything Dr. Mathew."

"I can take you home with me, Audrey. What do you say? Your aunties would be so happy!"

"I would love that, Jason."

The doctor smiled:

"Young love!" then added with his happy mood:

"Children, I will sort out the papers and then she is free to go. However I will give you some prescribed medication to help you with pain and you will have to contact your doctors if any more problems and your local hospital."

The doctor came near Audrey and shook her hand and more like whispering added to her:

"Never met such a kind lady like you and really inspired me. Thank you for your words. I wish you and this young man all the best."

Then turning around to me he looked serious and said as he was leaving:

"Look after her! You will not find another one like her."

A nurse came to help Audrey to dress and I went downstairs into the little hospital cafe and bought some sandwiches and drinks to take with us for the road and yes, fruit. Audrey loved fruit.

Took everything into the car and was ready to return up and pick her up and was thinking it was a good idea to call Lucy and Clara.

"Hi Jason. How is Audrey?"

"Well, the doctor released her to come home. Was thinking to let you know and we will be on our way back. Might take 3-4 hours. See how it goes. She will be so happy to be home."

I went to pick her up and a nurse prepared everything, a little language she had and my beautiful Audrey was in a wheelchair.

Saying goodbye, she saw many people she knew in a few days.

Finally we were in the car and ready to go.

I gently helped her to go into the front seat.

I put a little blanket on her legs and covered her gently.

She smiled at me and she said:

"Jason!"

"Yes, Audrey. We have sandwiches, fruit, and drinks. Anything you want… a bag full of food for us."

She touched my hand and I felt a bit confused and not sure what she wanted.

"Can I give you a hug!"

That surprised me and smiled. I came near her and she put her arm around my neck and could smell her hair. She was smelling like flowers.

"Thank you"

"Don't I get kisses?" I teased her.

"Maybe… just let me get better."

We were ready to go. I was driving and felt so happy that I had Audrey in the car with me and taking her back home.

As we drove back it was a long journey and Audrey seemed to get comfortable in her chair, more like falling asleep and cuddling a little blanket. She was still tired and recovering.

As we drove back on a big road, we got stuck in the traffic as if it was an accident. And it seemed to take quite a long time. It was getting dark in the evening and I got a bit anxious. Audrey was asleep and was not sure if I should drive back or stop again.

This was a new journey for me and a new adventure and I loved it. My life was totally on a new path and journey and I was determined to make things work, but I knew that all of those blessings were possible because of the Hand of the Lord.

Since I took a new path of love, faith, walking with the Lord, my life and perspective changed. Slowly things changed and even if I lost my mum, the Lord blessed me with a church, new friends and a new career path different shaped at work and so many more. But above all my heart met something that was forgotten, something that was buried. My heart started to fly again and I was following my heart. I was following love and I was driving back home with the woman of my dreams, a woman that I was in love with and I was ready to be with her and start a new family.

As the car was driving and I could see the lights of the town, I knew I was home. I knew I did the right thing, following the Spirit, following my heart.

We were home!

The End

Bible References

Proverbs 3:5-6
Trust in the LORD with all your heart, and do not lean on your own understanding. In all your ways acknowledge him, and he will make straight your paths.

Psalm 119:105
Your word is a lamp to my feet and a light to my path.

James 4:7
Submit yourself therefore to God. Resist the devil, and he will flee from you.

1 John 4:8
Anyone who does not love does not know God, because God is love.

2 Corinthians 5:17
Therefore, if anyone is in Christ, he is a new creation. The old has passed away, behold; the new has come.

Romans 12:2
Do not be conformed to this world, but be transformed by the renewal of your mind, that by testing you may discern what is the will of God, what is good and acceptable and perfect.

Psalm 23:4
Even though I was through the valley of the shadow of death, I will fear no evil, for you are with me; your rod and your staff they comfort me.

Joshua 1:8
This Book of the Law shall not depart from your mouth, but you shall meditate on it day and night, so that you may be careful to do according to all that is written in it. For then you will make your way prosperous, and then you will have good success.

John 4:24
God is spirit, and those who worship him must worship in Spirit and truth.

Romans 8:28
And we know that for those who love God all things work together for good, for those who are called according to his purpose.

Jeremiah 29:11
For I know the plans I have for you, declares the Lord, plans for welfare and not for evil, to give you a future and a hope.

John 1:14
And the word became flesh and dwelt among us, and we have seen his glory, glory as of the only Son from the Father, full of grace and truth.

1 John 2:15-17
Do not love the world or the things in the world. If anyone loves the world, the love of the Father is not in him. For all that is in the world - the desires of the flesh and the desires of the eyes and pride of life - is not from the Father but is from the world. And the world is passing along with its desires, but whoever does the will of God abides forever.

1 Corinthians 10:13
No temptation has overtaken you that is not common to man. God is faithful, and he will not let you be tempted beyond your ability, but with the temptation he will also provide the way of escape, that you may be able to endure it.

2 Timothy 3:16
All Scriptures are breathed out by God and profitable for teaching, for reproof, for correction, and for training in righteousness,

John 3:16-17
For God so loved the world, that he gave his only Son, that whoever believes in him should not perish but have eternal life. For God did not send his Son into the World to condemn the world, but in order that the world might be saved through him.

Romans 12:12
Rejoice in hope, be patient in tribulation, be constant in prayer.

Hebrews 10:36
For you have a need of endurance, so when you have done the will of God you may receive what is promised.

Galatians 6:9
And let us not grow weary in doing good, for in due season we will reap, if we do not give up.

Philippians 1:6
And I am sure of this, that he who began a good work in you will bring it to completion on the day of Jesus Christ.

Psalm 16:11
You make known to me the path of life; in your presence is fullness of joy; at your right hand are pleasures forevermore.

John 16:24
Until now you have not asked anything in my name. Ask, and you will receive, that your joy may be full.

Psalm 118:24
This is the day that the Lord has made; let us rejoice and be glad in it.

Galatians 5:22
But the fruit of the Spirit is love, joy, peace, patience, kindness, goodness, faithfulness, gentleness, self control; against such things there is no law.

1 Thessalonians 5:16-18
Rejoice always, pray without ceasing, give thanks in all circumstances; for this is the will of God in Christ Jesus for you.

Milton Keynes UK
Ingram Content Group UK Ltd.
UKHW010707280324
440307UK00001B/9